The Black
Wolf's Wedding

DAHLIA ROSE

The Black Wolf's Wedding

Chapter One

Ivy Bellefonte's Gallery Opening, Rustic Nights.

She trailed her hand along the gold embossed banner in admiration as the last of her paintings was hung. The Foxworth Gallery was the most well known in San Francisco, and she was having her first showing at the exclusive space. Her next showing would be at their sister gallery in New York but she wouldn't even think about that yet, it made her stomach tie in knots.

She was dressed and ready for the night an hour before anyone arrived, and Ivy smiled as her agent Bunny ordered around men twice her size from her petite five-foot-one frame. Her cell buzzed in the small clutch purse she carried. It matched the comfortable but trendy red shoes she wore while her black dress clung to her curves. She had loved how it looked against her ebony skin when she bought it, but now Ivy hoped it wasn't too revealing since the back consisted of only two small straps. With all her thoughts, Ivy barely got to answer the phone on the last ring without looking at the readout.

"Hey Baby girl, what time do me and Eric get there?" Her father's deep baritone voice boomed through speaker before she could even say hello. Ivy winced.

"Hi Dad, are you off work already?" Ivy said hesitantly. She really didn't want them there but she couldn't say hey family, don't show up.

"Well, you know how it is in the Kristoff district. They set the time, and today they needed the docks cleared early," her father answered.

Ivy sighed, knowing their options were limited. Their family was part of a culture that very few knew about. San Francisco was divided into four districts. The leader of each wolf clan took control of a district. Their father, Theo Bellefonte, while human, had aligned himself with wolves long before they were born and now they lived and worked under their laws.

"So what time, Kit-kat?" her father prodded again, using her childhood nickname.

"Hey Kit-kat!" she heard her brother's teasing yell.

"Tell Eric hey, and nine is good, Dad," Ivy said weakly.

"That's a ten-four, good buddy." Her father laughed at his own joke. "We'll be there at nine sharp."

She loved her father and brother but while everyone would show up dressed to the nines, the farthest they would go was to tuck their work shirts into their pants. They were beer drinkers, and she hoped after a few cold ones at the neighborhood bar they would forget about her opening and head on home.

Ivy felt bad for being ashamed of how they acted, but at another opening with other artists, they almost got into a brawl because someone said something negative about her work. Sometimes things didn't mix, and her father liked to point out they were diamonds in the rough. *Far, far in the rough,* she thought. She wanted to gnaw the nail polish off her new manicure as she worried. Tonight needed to go well. *Please, please, please,* Ivy sent up the silent prayer.

"You need this before you break out in hives."

An arm reached around her and handed her a glass of champagne that she took gratefully. Ivy turned to face her best friend Trent. He was dressed in a black tuxedo with a red silk bow tie and looked dapper. He was shorter and wiry with a smaller body structure. The way he dressed reminded her of a librarian sometimes. Trent was smart as a whip and had such a great personality with a sense of humor. Ivy always thought he needed someone intelligent and loving. She'd set him up a few times with women she knew but it never went anywhere.

He kissed her cheek and patted her shoulder. "Stop fretting, this will go marvelously."

She smiled at him gratefully. "From your lips to God's ears."

"Ivy, everything is amazing, you look gorgeous, this has been in the works for twelve weeks. I'm not going to jinx it by saying nothing will go wrong, but nothing will go wrong." Trent grinned.

Ivy slapped his arm. "You just jinxed it!"

"Then if it all falls apart, I owe you a Coke," Trent said.

"You owe me a Xanax," she replied and felt some of her tension ease with the friendly teasing between them.

Bunny came hurrying over, and Ivy looked at her agent dressed in a soft rose Chanel suit. *Do they make clothes that small or does she have her clothes specially tailored?* Ivy wondered. Her chignon was perfect, and her glasses perched on her tiny nose.

"It's show time darling, lets wow them with your talent!" Bunny said enthusiastically. "I'm going to open the doors. Go stand by your favorite piece and smile, answer questions, and be your fabulous self. Trent, freshen her champagne."

"Yes ma'am." Trent gave her a mock salute and went off to find one of the waiters hired for the night.

Ivy did what she was told and wanted to guzzle the drink in her hand instead of sipping at the bubbles. The gallery was filled with more people than she thought would come, art critics and the press, people whose Rolex or tennis bracelet was worth more money than she made the last year.

The loud music and the sound of talking seemed to dim when he walked into the gallery. Everyone, humans and shifters, knew Lazarus Vale. She had to ask his permission to start her business in his district. He was the alpha of his clan, and the three other districts had appointed him the leader of their consortium; everything began and ended with him. He was larger than life. His dark hair was styled and the silver gray shark-skin suit he wore had to be tailor made to fit his body that well. Ivy estimated his height at around six three, and his dark eyes scanned the room. Beside him stood one man and a woman, both wearing black and not smiling. The three of them caused everyone to stare, and she could tell they felt the same way she did… intimidated.

Bunny patted her arm frantically, and Ivy almost spilled her drink. "I never expected him to come. Darling, you are about to become a legend."

"Bunny... I don't think..."

She never got to finish her sentence because her agent had scurried off to follow the enigmatic Lazarus Vale. Other guests came up and spoke to her, asked about her work, and she talked to them pleasantly. All the while she watched him move from one piece of art to another. Every once in a while, he spoke to the woman whom Ivy assumed was his date, but they didn't look affectionate. In fact, the woman looked like she was suspicious of everyone and everything in the gallery.

"Well, well, the myth, the legend himself is here," Trent murmured from beside her.

"God knows why." Ivy took a sip of her champagne. "They don't look like they want to be here in the least."

"One should be pleased when he comes down from his ivory tower," Trent said. "Remember to bow and scrape to the wolf lord when he graces you with his presence."

Ivy giggled, and Lazarus Vale's head whipped around like he heard them, and he pinned both her and Trent with a dark look. His blue eyes were so intense, she almost forgot to breathe and Ivy's laughter dried up instantly when he walked towards her with purposeful strides.

"He couldn't have heard us, could he?" Trent shifted beside her nervously.

"I doubt it with all the noise in here," Ivy said but doubted her words. Wolves were known for exceptional hearing. But here he came, and his entourage kept up with his pace.

"Ms. Bellefonte," he said, the timber of his voice sending goose bumps along her skin.

"Very nice of you to attend my small showing, Mr. Vale," Ivy said.

"I like to keep an eye on what's going on in my district," Lazarus answered. "Have a good evening, Ms. Bellefonte, I'm sure we'll be speaking again."

He turned and walked away, and Ivy watched as a waiter ran up with a drink in a tumbler glass. Lazarus took it and sipped before nodding his approval to the waiter who left as quickly as he came.

"What the hell was that?" Trent whispered.

Ivy shook her head slowly. "I have no clue."

The night progressed, and as people filtered out, she thought soon she would be able to go home and take off her heels. *Spoke too soon*, Ivy thought as Bunny hurried up to her.

"I know I said you could leave in a minute,

but before you do, you have to go say thank you to Mr. Vale. He bought five of your larger pieces," Bunny gushed.

"Why?" Ivy asked.

Bunny looked at her, shocked. "Because you're the artist, and he likes your work. How much champagne did you have tonight?"

"I understand that, Bunny, but he didn't seem impressed," Ivy said. "Never mind. I'll go say thank you and make you happy."

"That's all I ever ask." Bunny walked away, muttering to herself about artists living in the clouds.

Ivy firmed her shoulders and took a deep breath before walking over to where Lazarus Vale stood. His entourage moved a discreet distance from him as she approached.

"Mr. Vale, Bunny told me you bought a few of my pieces. Thank you, I hope you enjoy them," Ivy said pleasantly.

"Art is art, I'll find someplace to put them," he said casually. "And the name is Lazarus. I'm not that formal unless I'm in the boardroom.

His word about art soured her instantly. "Well, Lazarus, why buy the art if it doesn't interest you? In fact, why come?"

"I came to see if you were a charlatan passing off stick figures and splattered paint as art," he said mildly. "When you formally asked me for sanctuary in my district, I wasn't sure I should give it to you."

"Then why did you?" she asked through gritted teeth.

"Your father and brother seem suited to the docks, you did not," Lazarus answered. "I was protecting you from any old dog being able to mount you." He cast a glance at Owen. "You still managed to align yourself with a mutt, a baseborn mind you."

"Lowest of the low, his mother probably was a German shepherd," the female of Lazarus's group commented as she passed and elegantly plucked a glass of champagne from a tray the waiter held. Her words made Lazarus and the other man laugh.

"Trent's line may not be as pure as yours but he doesn't expect anything from me," Ivy snapped, hating the way this disparaged her friend. "You should by no means buy anything not worthy of your ivory tower."

"You seem to forget, I make the decision of what's worthy or not. Even if I buy it, the damn things may sit in my closets catching dust with other objects I get bored with." Lazarus smiled.

"You can take your..." Ivy saw Bunny's face and controlled her temper. "It's your decision to make, again thank you for admiring my work." She stepped closer so only he could hear. "Now admire my damn ass as I leave your egomaniacal presence."

Trent walked over to her as she walked away from Lazarus. "Everything okay?"

"The Lord and master wanted to tell me exactly what he feels about my art," Ivy seethed. "He's the biggest dick in the world."

Trent stayed by her side the rest of the night but she could still feel Lazarus's eyes on her every step. Instead of leaving, she ended up staying until the lights were out in the gallery. The air was cold when she stepped outside, and she pulled the wrap over her shoulders against the chill.

"You can wait here, and I'll get the car if you give me…" Trent never got to finish the sentence.

The sound of menacing growls emanated from the darkness, and the body of a wolf appeared. Ivy could already tell he wasn't a pure blood. His coloring was off, and his fur was long and short in some places and missing in others.

"Trent, is it one of the baseborn?" Ivy asked slowly, keeping her eyes on the beast.

"I really hate that name but yes, it's one of us," Trent muttered.

"Can you talk to it, see what it wants?" Ivy

whispered harshly.

"What, bark at it?" Trent asked incredulously. "I'm not part of that world."

"You can't shift and defend us?" Ivy wanted to know.

"I very rarely shift anymore. It seems too uncivilized," Trent whined. "That means undressing and…"

"Ugh! Forget it Owen, we need to get out of here fast. I will slip out of my shoes slowly, and when I say 'move' we haul ass." Ivy spoke from the corner of her mouth.

As soon as she said the words, Ivy saw the idea wasn't going to work. The baseborn wolf moved toward them. Its growl became louder, and he showed menacing teeth. The intent was clear—they were in serious danger, and Trent shook beside her, just as scared as she was. She kept forgetting he wasn't an alpha and hated his second nature. He was even less help than she was. Ivy lifted her leg slowly so she could slip her heels off and held one in her hand to use as a weapon. It wouldn't kill the mangy thing but maybe she could wound it or get her heel in its bloodshot eyes. When it attacked, instead of using her "shoe weapon," she screamed and tried to protect her face.

The first bite never came. Instead, she heard a

yelp, and when she slowly turned Ivy saw what had saved them. A wolf was now protecting them, one that was pure black and five times bigger than the baseborn that attacked. The yellow eyes of their savior looked at her while the baseborn shook its head from the blow it received. The baseborn turned his attention to the black wolf. Its gnashing teeth were easily deflected, and the black wolf caught it around the neck and shook it like a rag between its strong jaws. The black wolf tossed the baseborn aside once more, and this time it ran away with a howling yelp. Silence reigned, and the black wolf stood watching them before the realization of who it was dawned on her.

"Mr. Vale… Lazarus?" Ivy asked hesitantly. The wolf gave a nod of its head and continued to stand there, silently waiting. "I think he's waiting for us to get to the car safely before he leaves."

"I-I'll go get the car if you give me the… the… you know metal things," Trent stammered like he was unable to think.

Ivy took the ring of keys from her clutch with trembling fingers without taking her eyes off the yellow gaze of Lazarus's wolf. Trent took them from her hand and scurried down the block, leaving her alone with the massive black wolf.

"Thank you, I guess… for being here."

Remnants of her fear caused her words to tremble.

She certainly didn't expect him to return to human form and say you're welcome. Seeing Lazarus naked would be disconcerting to say the least. Standing by a gallery with a wolf close by was definitely not how she expected her night to end. Finally, Ivy breathed a sigh of relief when the lights of her car came around the corner and Trent was behind the wheel. He pulled to the curb in her Miata convertible and by the time she got in the passenger seat and looked to where the wolf was standing it was gone.

"That was unreal," Trent said.

Ivy nodded. "You're telling me."

All the way back to her apartment, she thought about the black wolf and Lazarus, trying to correlate the man and the beast as one person. The man had rubbed her the wrong way, and the wolf stood to protect her. Ivy wondered how it was that she liked the animal more than the man and smiled as she answered her own question. The wolf couldn't talk.

Chapter Two

Ivy Bellefonte, if she only knew what was within her, what power she possessed, Lazarus mused as he drove. Usually he had at least two of his clan with him because there was more to the darkness than just wolves and the clans they led. Humans were at the bottom of the food chain, and they didn't even know. Right now, he had an appointment to keep and an offer to make. One that would not be well received, but he loved a challenge. It was more fun that way. He'd called Kristoff for permission to enter his territory, and the conversation showed him that some other clans seemed to be getting too big for the boots he'd tailored for them. He played the conversation back in his mind as he maneuvered the Mercedes through the inclined roads of San Francisco.

"Kristoff, this is—"

Kristoff cut his words off. "Lazarus, I know who this is. How are you, my friend?"

He gritted his teeth, hating being cut off but keeping his voice mild. "This is a courtesy call to let you know I will be in your district. When you sense it, it's just me."

"And why are you in my district... old friend?" Kristoff's voice changed to wariness and curiosity. "No business goes on in my area without my say so."

"Luckily, it's not business and like I said this is a courtesy call," Lazarus's tone also changed to his serious don't-fuck-with-me voice.

"Why make rules if you are just going to break them yourself?" Kristoff snapped. "It seems you only follow your own directives when you want."

"Let me put it this way, Kristoff. If it was something you needed to know, you would," Lazarus snapped. "Remember your place before I put you in another."

"If you recall, a vote could be cast...."

"And what, who will challenge me to lead?" Lazarus heard the wolf in his voice and tried to control his anger. "Try it, and you could end up begging scraps from the baseborn, and that's if I let you live. You've been given notice that I am in your district, if I sense any of yours snooping around I'll snap its neck and leave its carcass on the steps of your house."

With those words he hung up and continued on his journey. At the next meeting of the clans, Lazarus knew he would have to jerk the chains back and remind them who was the one who united the clans and gave them each some semblance of power. It was within him to break the faction but he didn't want to rule like his father. He was also tired of being alone, and this was the reason for going to the docks. He hated the place, the smell of it, the house and warehouses.

He pulled his Mercedes besides a beat-up red truck and looked at the house with a sigh. It was a trailer, double-wide with a small patch of yellow grass as a front yard and between mismatched houses with peeling paint. They were all in varying stages of semi rundown condition, and the mailbox had *Bellefonte* written on it in sloppy white painted letters. He knocked and stepped back, and when the door opened it creaked. Lazarus winced at the sound.

"Come on in, she's on her way. Dad is in the back." The kid took a bite of his sandwich and stepped aside so Lazarus could enter.

Eric Bellefonte had to be around twenty-four or so, and compared to Lazarus he was a babe in infancy when it came to age. He was tall and gangly, wearing faded torn jeans and a well-worn blue t-shirt. Like Ivy, his hair was black yet his skin tone as at least a few shades darker. Eric didn't seem to give a shit about who he was. Lazarus looked around the interior of the home.

The saggy old couch and recliner seemed out of place with the forty-six-inch flat screen TV. He knew that on their salary they couldn't afford a few things in the house like the surround sound and the fancy coffee, cappuccino maker.

It was an easy assumption that Ivy probably gave them money, and the knowledge made his anger burn. They were men, they should live by their own means and not wait for the female to take care of them. As he stood in the middle of the living room, the back door opened with the same noisy creak and an older version of Eric stepped in, wiping his hands. Theo Bellefonte had a gray, low cut beard against his dark skin and wore a cap pulled down over his unkempt hair.

"You are early, Mr. Vale, excited to see my girl, huh?" Theo said with a smile and a nod.

Eric could hear the hint of a Caribbean accent in his voice. It had been dulled by the years he had lived in the United States. But unlike Ivy and her brother Eric who were born there, his accent was still clear while they had none.

"Let's hope this goes as well as we both want it to," Lazarus said. "At the gallery opening she was attacked by the baseborn. If she aligns with me, she is protected as well as both of you."

"But we still work the docks?" Eric said. "Or do we get an upgrade in our living situation?"

Lazarus turned to the boy and growled. "You want to upgrade your life on the back of your sister?"

"He means no disrespect, Mr. Vale," Theo said quickly. "He understands that what he wants must be earned."

"The man is worth millions, Dad! Ivy lives like the princess, and what am I?" Eric shot back.

Lazarus wanted to beat the boy to within an inch of his life but he needed this to go well. "You want an upgrade in your life status? Fine, from Monday you will have a new apartment, a new job being the supervisor in one of my warehouses. Your father will become the manager of this warehouse, and you will have a salary increase. There will be money deposited into your bank account, enough for a good nest egg." Lazarus met both their gazes with his cold one. "But know this: you blow the money, you get lax on the job and my profits decreases, you will lose it all and you are back here, am I clear?"

"As the blue sky above." Eric took a huge bite of his sandwich with a smug grin on his face. Lazarus wanted to dislike him but he knew the impetuous nature of youth, so he let it go.

"Do you want a beer while you wait?" Theo invited. "Please have a seat."

"No thank you to the beer." Lazarus stood

with his hands clasped behind his back and looked at the furniture. He wondered if his massive frame would break the old chair and decided to stand. He made a mental note to make sure the apartment was furnished. "I'll stand."

In a few minutes he heard another car drive up and the door slam.

"Dad, Eric, why is there a Mercedes outside your house?" Ivy called out. When she opened the door and saw him standing there, she stopped dead in her tracks. "Why is he here?"

"Kit-kat, why didn't you tell us you were attacked by a baseborn?" Theo said.

"Dad, it was nothing," Ivy muttered. Lazarus could smell the wariness coming off her.

"She hangs out with that baseborn geek, Trent," Eric piped in.

Ivy pointed her finger at him. "Don't call him a geek, Eric, you ass."

"Both of you stop," Theo ordered. "I need you safe, Ivy."

"I am safe," she said and listened as her father said something in patois.

Lazarus knew it was the native language of St Lucia, and it was a broken French creole. But understanding it was another thing. Whatever Theo said started an intense back and forth conversation between her and her father. She was fluent in the foreign language and spoke to her father in a hard clipped tone. Like him, Eric looked confused about what they were saying. He took that moment to assess her; she was more than he ever expected.

Her hair was pulled up into a high ponytail, and the streak of white stood out in the dark tresses. Ivy was dressed in workout capris with an orange stripe down the sides. She wore an orange tank under an oversized white t-shirt that hung off her shoulders. Her skin seemed to shimmer like bronze in the sun, and more than once she cast her intense hazel eyed gaze in his direction.

He'd never seen a black woman with eyes like hers. Ivy was unique and more than he thought possible. His wolf agreed because he felt the instinctual urge to claim her. To pin her to his bed and fuck her from behind then bite her neck — not too savagely, but enough so they would know who was her mate. The thought made his cock jump in his pants and he growled. It was loud enough that it made them all go silent and look at him.

"I didn't come here to argue," Lazarus snapped. "The proposition has been made to you, Theo Bellefonte, from the leader of the Vale clan. Do you accept?"

Theo nodded. "*Wi,* I accept."

Ivy looked from Lazarus to her father. "Exactly what is going on, what proposition?"

Theo sighed and took her hand. "Ivy, my darling girl, I am doing what's best for you."

"And that is?" she asked slowly.

"Mr. Vale has asked to be mated with you, and I have accepted on your behalf," her father answered.

She shook her head. "You did what now?"

"I proposed a marriage between you and me, your father accepted," Lazarus said mildly. "We are betrothed."

"The hell we are," she snapped. "We are not betrothed, be anything. I refuse."

"You can't, your father has given his blessings," Lazarus said.

"This isn't the 1600s. I have a right to say no, and I just did." Ivy put her hand on her hips and glared at them.

"Don't blow this for us," Eric said. "Ivy, he's going to give us new jobs and a new swanky place to live, even money in our accounts."

She glared at her brother. "You're selling me like cattle, or a whore, so you can get some cash? My dowry is to set you and Dad up like kings?"

"Not like kings, trust me, they will work," Lazarus said mildly.

Ivy turned her furious glance to Lazarus. "Well la de dah, the lord and master Lazarus Vale gives the Bellefonte family his blessing by marrying the daughter. Did anyone fucking ask you to do that?"

"Language, Ivy, please," Theo begged.

"Go to hell, all of you. I thought you loved me, dad. I do as much as I can for you, for Eric, and still you sell me off." Lazarus saw tears fall from her hazel eyes, and she swiped them away furiously. "I'll leave this damn town and start somewhere else before I marry him, so you all can go... go... suck an egg."

Ivy slammed out of the house, and the engine of her car roared to life.

"Well that went better than I expected," Lazarus said.

Theo shook his head. "I doubt she will change her mind, Mr. Vale. She is very obstinate, my Ivy. Maybe it's best to call this off."

"By no means, this is exactly what I want, she is what I want," Lazarus said with a grin. "Nothing good is ever easily attained. This is a battle I intend to win."

"You're a glutton for punishment," Eric said.

"Maybe I am."

He left feeling better than he had in a long time. Not much fascinated him anymore but now he'd found his mate. In his head, the wolf within howled, anticipating the chase. There was no doubt that Ivy would be his when she found out who she truly was. He would be by her side.

He found her at her studio much later that evening. It was easy enough to get inside since the building was his and he knew the master code to all his properties. He scented her from behind the door, and a low growl of arousal emanated from his lips. Lazarus knew he had to take it slow, especially with her. His closest enforcers had told him that sometimes he could be… brutish. Somehow he doubted very much that tactic would work with Ivy. Lazarus knocked on the door of the converted warehouse. Loud, angry music came from behind the barrier, and he grimaced.

He was more of a classic rock man himself. He doubted very much she could hear his knock above the screeching words and electric guitar so he used his fist to pound the door before looking around the painted walls of the hallway. His construction people had done good work with this conversion, and he noted she had taken the farthest loft on the top floor so she wouldn't bother anyone with her music. That and the sound proofing probably made her the dream tenant for the other residents of the lofts. The music finally turned off, and he turned to the door, waiting for it to open.

Ivy drew it back, and he heard the weight of the thick wooden frame glide against the metal tracks. She didn't just look angry, she glowered at him, probably a combination of his interruption and the events at her father's house. There was a smudge of blue paint on her chocolate brown cheek and white on her nose, and her hair was now in a messy bun on her head. A cute picture if she wasn't shooting daggers at him with her eyes.

"What do you want?" Ivy snapped impolitely.

"I came to see how you were doing," Lazarus replied smoothly. "Also, maybe you'd like to go to dinner with me?"

"I ate," she said.

"Can we talk?" Lazarus smiled, hoping it would make her lower her defenses.

"No."

"Christ, you are a hard nut to crack," Lazarus said in exasperation.

"Well, when someone tells you that you're forced to marry him, and her family sells her out, you can see how I'd be moody," Ivy replied.

"Let's talk about it," Lazarus implored. "Can I come in and we talk?"

"I said no."

"I own the building…" Lazarus let the words trail off.

Ivy screamed in angry frustration. "Of course, because I can't even live fucking anywhere, eat, sleep, work or do anything without the Vale say so."

She turned on her heels and stomped away, leaving the door open. Lazarus took that as an invitation to follow and stepped inside her workspace. He could already tell that this was her studio and her home. She went with a rustic, simple theme for décor and kept the main area of the apartment primarily empty except for an overstuffed couch and an armchair for sitting. The bay window held multicolored cushions, and an afghan was thrown over it as if it was her favorite place to sit and watch the city.

From that position, she could also see the wall mounted flat screen TV on the half exposed brick wall. A glance through the open bedroom door told him she kept all her favorite things there, and it was more of her personal space than anything else. He wondered if she still had a jewelry box from when she was a teen on her dresser and what kind of naughty undies she kept hidden from the world. Mostly the area was filled with canvases, paints, and a few easels. The apartment hosted a medium sized kitchenette; he saw a coffee pot and a wine fridge and wondered if there was anything to eat in the actual fridge. There was evidence of her work in partial stages around the loft.

They were all magnificent even though many were uncompleted. Lazarus assumed she worked on a piece when the inspiration struck her. He turned to where she stood in front of a large canvas that he estimated to be at least eight feet tall. In the middle was a silhouette of a woman. The lines and curves on her body were sensual and oozed sex appeal. Behind and across the silhouette were angry swatches of colors. She threw vivid blue colors from the tip of the brush onto the canvas and then feathered the tip with a brush with spread bristles. Watching her in action was even more breathtaking, but she was using the task to ignore him.

"It's not polite to ignore your guest," Lazarus said.

"You own the building, you're not my guest," Ivy replied without looking at him. "I don't want to marry you."

"No kidding. A guy could be insulted," Lazarus drawled.

"You should be, you're not my type," Ivy shot back.

He gritted his teeth. "I see that from the caliber of company you keep."

She whirled and glared at him. "You see, it's that uppity look down your nose attitude about people. That's why people don't like you."

In her anger and expressive hand gestures, she managed to whip blue paint at him, and it spattered on his suit as she spoke. They both saw the effect, and he looked down on the big blue droplets on the dark blue fabric.

"Sorry." She covered her mouth with her fingers but he could see her lips twitch with a smile and laughter in her eyes.

"This is a two thousand dollar suit," Lazarus said in irritation.

"Oh boo-hoo, it's an artist's studio. That's like doing construction and not expecting to get dirty." Ivy rolled her eyes. "It's acrylic, it will wash out, pretty boy."

"It doesn't have the same affect as on your canvas. The sensual lines you created aren't meant for a designer suit." Lazarus looked at the spots wondering if he should try to clean them or take the jacket to the cleaners.

"You sound like you know what you're talking about." Ivy went to the kitchen and came back with a wet cloth. "Don't just look at it, dab. It won't damage the fancy-schmancy fabric."

Lazarus took the towel and did as she directed. "I like art, and yours is very good. You talk about my being elitist but listen to how you talk in regard to people with money."

Ivy laughed incredulous. "It is so not the same, you were born with a silver spoon in your mouth, and us mortals work for everything we have."

"I've worked damn hard for what's mine," Lazarus growled angrily. "Not a penny I spend I haven't earned. Just because I don't work on the docks or dress in a cheap suit at your gallery opening doesn't mean I don't know work."

"Jeez, leave Trent out of this," Ivy demanded. "The fact that you feel the need to talk down about him shows that we are not a good match. You are the alpha of your clan, and of course you'd expect me to give up friendships and the likes because of you. Wrong buddy, I may work in your district but I don't want to be part of your ivory tower. I'm not even attracted to you."

"We should test that theory." Lazarus strode toward her and grabbed her shoulders and pulled her against him. Instantly, he wanted to strip her naked and take her on the floor. He lowered his head to nuzzle her neck, and when she shuddered, he chuckled in satisfaction. "I can smell your arousal, between the pain and the perfume. You would taste like a ripe plum against my tongue and I could make you feel things, such hot, intense fucking things. Till you scream in pleasure and beg for more."

He kissed his way across her cheek, and he was just about to sample the sweet fruit of Ivy Bellefonte when the door slid open and an annoying voice made him grit his teeth.

"Ivy," Trent sang out, "I got your favorite moo-shu pork with the fried rice and of course dump…"

He stopped when he saw them standing in the middle of the room. Lazarus held her tighter against him as if Trent being there threatened his mate. Something about that chimera mutt rubbed him the wrong way, more than his lineage. There was something off.

"You're interrupting us," Lazarus snapped. "Go away, baseborn."

"You don't order me around," Trent tried to say bravely but Lazarus could sense his fear.

Lazarus bared his teeth in a growl, let her go, and moved toward Owen. "Yet another theory to test. I'll snap you like a twig mutt."

"Lazarus, leave him alone," Ivy ordered.

"Trent, you weren't interrupting anything, Lazarus was just leaving."

He turned to face her. "Was I now?"

She met his eyes with her hazel gaze and said defiantly, "Yes you were, good night."

Lazarus nodded, deciding it was best not to show his hand just yet. For now he would play the game even though he wanted to pick his teeth with the baseborn mutt she called a friend.

"This isn't over," Lazarus said and turned his attention to Trent. "She has been mated to me — you touch her, I will know. I will scent it in the air, and I will snap your neck and throw you to my people as a pet. A ragged, torn little mutt for their pups to chew on."

"I'm not your..." Ivy began to say.

But Lazarus was already striding toward the door. He sensed when someone breeched the lines of his district without consent, and while he could send his enforcers to take care of the problem, he felt the need to get his aggression out.

In his car, he pressed the Bluetooth phone feature, and the husky voice answered almost immediately.

"Silvia, before you say anything, I sensed it as well. I am on my way. Get Luca, we are going on the hunt," Lazarus said briskly.

"We'll be waiting," she replied and hung up.

Lazarus glanced at the building one more time, wanting to go back in but business came first. He couldn't seem weak or lapse in protecting what was his. There would be time to deal with the baseborn and implement an investigation. Till then it was time to show whoever dared tread in his district that Lazarus Vale was the last person they wanted to fuck with.

Chapter Three

She'd signed up to teach a series of dinner, wine, and paint classes for couples, friends, and those unattached. They were held and local restaurants where the upstairs room was made private and easels were set up. Ivy loved these relaxed informal gatherings, the playfulness of the couples. Sometimes one or two shy women reminded Ivy of herself. She was thirty years old, and at an early age, she learned too soon her mother wasn't coming back.

Ivy also learned that her father wasn't the strong man or provider that she and Eric needed. There was school, then home to clean and make sure they ate. It was the same in college and with her art—whatever money she made had to take care of them all, even now. *Until they sold me out for an apartment and a bank account*, Ivy shook her head angrily to push the thoughts away. She pasted a smile on her face as her student guests arrived.

When most had arrived, she smiled. "Welcome to a night of fun. Who's ready to paint?"

They all clapped and chattered among themselves while appetizers and drinks were served, and she explained the paint pallets before them and gave them just a hint of direction. It was more about having fun than technique, but Ivy was always delighted to have raw talent in their ranks.

"Remember, don't worry about doing it right or wrong. There's none of that here, just have fun," Ivy encouraged with a smile and took a sip of her own wine. "Paint what's in your mind's eye, and just let it flow from your finger to the tip of your brush."

"I've seen your work, Ms. Bellefonte. Are you going to paint something today?" one woman asked excitedly. "I couldn't get in to your gallery opening, the reviews say it's marvelous."

"I'll dabble today as well," Ivy said. "The gallery will have my work for another three weeks if you still want to go see it. It has public days on Wednesdays. Let's paint, ladies and gents."

Ivy liked when people appreciated her work. Not the pretentious ones who lifted their noses and pulled out a checkbook to own the latest thing not knowing the background behind it, the motivation. As she walked around giving people hints here and there on shading, shadows, or highlights, she noticed one man with his canvas hiding his face. *Obviously shy,* Ivy thought, delighted. She adored the shy ones and always gave them extra help.

"Hiding behind the canvas..." her words halted when she saw who was sitting there. Lazarus Bellefonte.

"What are you doing here?" Ivy said low under her breath.

"Enjoying a night of fine food and letting my artistic bird fly." He took a sip from a glass of red wine, and the slender crystal stem seemed all too fragile in his large hand.

Ivy smirked. "Artistic bird?"

"My inspiration knows no boundaries," Lazarus replied smoothly. "Look at what I did."

She came around and peered at his drawing and held back her laughter. Lazarus drew a stick figure sailor wearing a triangle hat holding a spy scope. The sea was blue wavy lines, and the sun was yellow, drawn like a child had done it. Ivy wondered for a moment if he was making fun of her craft but she doubted it very much. She knew he was using this as a funny segue into a conversation since their last few had ended so badly.

"As you can see, this image portrays my adventurous nature and the love of the sea," Lazarus said in a serious tone.

Ivy nodded. "Yes, the ocean seems to come alive beneath his boat that possibly is a triangle, or well, some shape."

"He is the crafter of his fate and his boat," Lazarus answered before he scribbled his name on the bottom. "There, a signed Vale piece. You can buy it for a thousand dollars."

Ivy sputtered laughter. "The point of this class is to make something you want to take home and hang on your wall."

"Ms. Bellefonte, can you show me how to shadow my clouds," one of her guests called from the front of the room.

"I have to go, Mr. Vale. You can't have all my attention all night," Ivy said.

"I'm Mr. Vale, am I? Since our conversation has to end, spend the day with me tomorrow, see that I'm not the big bad wolf," Lazarus suggested.

Ivy leaned closer. "You are the big bad wolf, and everyone in our world knows it."

He moved so they were practically nose-to-nose. "Scared?"

"Never." Ivy found that that she enjoyed the back and forth between them and Lazarus was charming. Did she have the wrong impression about him after all?

"Ten a.m. in front of your apartment," Lazarus said with a wicked grin.

Ivy's heart skipped a beat in excitement. "I'll see you then."

The rest of the night passed quickly, and she noticed when Lazarus's people came in with a quick nod he left. It was the woman from the night of the gallery opening and the same man. Neither of them smiled, and she wondered exactly what was wrong and what they did for Lazarus. Even though the girl was gorgeous as hell, she looked dangerous and deadly. The wine and paint session had been a great success, and before she left, the manager of the restaurant asked her if she'd be willing to schedule a few more. Ivy told him to contact Bunny, and she headed home for the night.

The next day she looked into the mirror and blew out a nervous breath. Why did he excite her so much even though she didn't like his boorish, highbrow behavior? What inside her seemed to tingle and grow like something trying to crawl out of her skin each time he was close? The sensation was close to pleasure and almost pain. Was this a carnal attraction she was feeling?

The questions bothered her but while her mind screamed danger, her body was flushed with excitement. The conversation she had with

Trent didn't make her feel much better, but just as she didn't like Lazarus's way of bullying his way through everything, she didn't like when Trent whined to have his way. It was childish and unappealing in a man even though he was her best friend.

"I don't get why you have to go. You see how he treats everyone?" Trent said petulantly.

"He deserves his say as much as the next guy. I work in his district, and even if we can be friends, or at least civil, it will be a good thing," Ivy explained calmly.

"Sure, like that's all he wants. If I hadn't walked into your studio... you guys were practically about to—" He never got to finish his comment.

"Trent, you're my best friend, and I love you, but what I was about to do or not do has nothing to do with you," Ivy said in a voice that bode no more discussion. She didn't mention that Lazarus wanted her to marry him, that would send Trent into a tailspin, and he'd break out in hives.

"All I'm saying is be careful. A man like Lazarus Vale always has an ulterior motive," Trent reminded her.

"As far as I know so does everyone in the world," Ivy murmured. "Anyway, I'm going to get going, call you late tonight, bye love ya."

She hung up during Trent's muttering and shook her head. He was being over protective but she was already wary so he didn't need to keep reminding her. What would have happened if Trent hadn't come over with food that night? A warmth spread through her as thoughts of Lazarus's kiss or his touch caused definite arousal. *Put them out of your head, Missie,* Ivy warned herself. Lazarus never said what they were doing so Ivy went with a relaxed look. It was Saturday, and she decided to wear a baseball jersey style long sleeve shirt in red and white that read *happy* across the front.

She'd pulled her dark hair into pigtails and frowned at the white streak. It had been there from birth and no matter what color she used it never held the dye. Ivy pulled a baseball cap on and with blue jeans and red sneakers completed her look. She applied a soft nude lip-gloss to her lips and shoved her cell phone, ID, and some cash into her wristlet purse. Going out didn't mean she was going to stupidly leave home without money. If her interaction with Lazarus was any clue as to how the day may end up, she might need to take a cab home. Ivy took the elevator downstairs from her apartment to wait for Lazarus at 9:55 a.m. True to his word, he was pulled up to the curb at ten exactly and stepped out of the car.

Lazarus's version of casual was a loose, blue men's v-neck sweater that stretched across the wide expanse of his chest with the sleeves pushed up to his forearms. He also wore tailored pants and shoes that were polished until they gleamed in the sunlight. Ivy admitted to herself the man was scrumptious and the looks other women gave him just reaffirmed her own assessment. He pushed his sunglasses back against dark hair and looked at her as she approached the car.

"Aren't you all peaches and cream delicious," he drawled. "You look good enough to eat."

"We'll have none of that," Ivy said firmly. "This is a let's get to know each other kind of day."

"I agree. Since we are to be married, we should know more about the person we will be spending the rest of our lives with." Lazarus walked around to open her car door. "I'm a Scorpio and was born under a full moon."

Ivy laughed. "I wouldn't expect anything less."

She slid into the car and looked at the sleek interior, Corinthian leather seats and gadgets and buttons on the dashboard that she knew nothing about. Her little Miata was a second-hand splurge, and his Mercedes convertible appeared to be made specifically for him and rolled off the line to be sent to his house.

"Must be nice to live in the lap of luxury," she commented when he got in the driver's side.

"You know how you call me elitist?" Lazarus said as he started the car. "Well, you're a middle-class snob, thumbing your nose at the rich. Everything I own I've earned."

"Many of us didn't have the name or the money behind us like you did," Ivy pointed out.

"Anyone in my pack will tell you and the records will show that I left on my own without my father or the Vale name to make my own way," Lazarus said as he maneuvered his way to the San Francisco traffic. "By the time my father died and I took leadership of the pack, I was self made and integrated my company into this life."

"So ambition made you such an ass sometimes?" Ivy asked bluntly.

He laughed. It was a pleasant sound that she didn't expect. "To lead the pack one cannot be weak. I'm fair and I'm blunt. I will do what needs to be done to make sure my pack survives and that the other districts know I am the top of the food chain."

"The baseborn certainly know that," she muttered.

He glanced at her. "Yes they do, and for a man who said he doesn't run with those of his blood your baseborn friend has certainly twisted your thinking of how they are unfairly treated."

"Trent works hard. He only mentioned how they have to stay in the poorest sections of town. The work is what none of the other clans want, and they are working for scraps," Ivy defended.

"Did he mention why the baseborn live the lives they lead, what they have done throughout the years to cause the districts to show them disfavor?" Lazarus asked. "You should ask him about their history sometime, or better yet, read it for yourself. The record takers have no side and show no favorites, they only document the truth."

"I've heard of them. One of each that is taken from birth, so they know only each other and are raised to watch and write the history," Ivy said with interest. "I honestly thought that was a myth."

"It's not, and maybe you'll want to read about your family," Lazarus commented casually.

"Who wants to read about the humans who beg for favors in the districts?" Ivy shrugged. "Our lives mean nothing in the grand scheme of things. We are only pawns in a game bigger than we can ever imagine."

"If you say so," Lazarus said noncommittally. "Enough of this discussion. It's making you tense, and that's not what today's about."

"Okay, so where are we going first?" Ivy said, willing to give him the benefit of the doubt for the day.

"Breakfast and then a boat ride out to Alcatraz for the tour and Pier 39," he said. "We're going to be tourists for the day, and if you're nice, you might get ice cream."

"I'll try to be very good, then," Ivy teased.

The soft growl that escaped him made gooseflesh erupt across her skin before he spoke softly. "Remember, you want me to not be the big bad wolf today and gobble you up. Don't give me incentives to do otherwise."

"I'll keep that in mind." Ivy shifted in her seat.

The rest of the ride was made with very little words between them. They ate breakfast at a small diner close to the Pier and Ivy liked the comfortable silence with conversation thrown in here and there. Ivy didn't mind not talking, and it was one of her pet peeves when out with Trent—he never stopped talking. Every meal was filled with words and conversation when sometimes all she wanted was some quiet. After breakfast, they walked over to where they would take the ferry to Alcatraz.

Again, walking in companionable silence and all he did was smile as he helped her onto the boat. *Hush, stop comparing them,* she admonished herself. Trent was her friend and God knows what Lazarus was. He wanted her to be his mate, and along with them being so completely opposite there was the fact of her being human and him being a wolf. She doubted very much his pack would have a human as their beta. The boat pulled away from the pier and the wind almost took the cap from her head. Lazarus's quick reflexes saved it, and he put it on backwards on her head.

He leaned forward and spoke into her ear over the sound of the boat. "I can see the wheels turning in your head. Remember, relaxed day."

"I'm not over thinking anything, I promise." Ivy smiled, and she could tell he didn't believe her. She quickly changed the subject. "I've always been apprehensive about going over to the island. I hear it's haunted."

"It more than likely is; are you scared of the unknown?" Lazarus asked.

Somehow it felt like his statement had a double meaning, and she chose her words wisely. "The thought of seeing a ghost is definitely not on my to-do list. Or the disembodied voices… Creepy."

"So a night tour or sleep over is out of the question?" he teased.

"I would swim home," Ivy said firmly. "Hey,

what am I talking about? I wouldn't agree to a nighttime anything on that island."

"Scaredy cat."

Ivy punched him lightly on the shoulder. "Don't be a jerk just because you're a big black wolf and you're not afraid of anything."

"Maybe some things," Lazarus said mildly.

She gave him a curious look. "Care to elaborate?"

He tweaked her nose. "I don't know you well enough for that yet."

She rubbed the area that he touched. "Why did you do that?"

"You're peaches and cream cute, I just had to," he said.

"You can be very charming when you want to," she pointed out. "If people saw this side of you more often, they'd be less prone to think you're mean."

"This side is for very few people to see." Lazarus met her gaze, and she felt like she was drowning in his intense blue eyes. "More often than not kindness is taken for weakness, and an alpha can never be seen as weak."

Ivy nodded. "I can see that. I could never understand why my father decided that we were safer in your world. I can't even fathom what you deal with, but I get it, as a leader your strength has to be public at all times. It seems like a lonely way to live."

"Not if you share it with me," Lazarus replied.

She let his words hang in the air, unable to answer or understand the raging emotions within her. Ivy still wondered why he would want a human mate when more suitable shifters were out there. Like the sleek woman who was always by his side, she would be a formidable mate for Lazarus, so why her? Ivy admitted to herself she was afraid of the answer and of everything that was happening in her life since he showed up at her gallery opening.

The tour of the prison island proved to be informative but the hollow halls with cells covered in peeling paint and cracked walls seemed more ominous. Ivy swore she heard whispers and saw shadows, and while she enjoyed the tour, she was glad to be off that rock. It felt ominous, as if eyes watched her from a distance. She shuddered at the thought.

The Pier was more fun. The crowds of people and the warm sun soothed the dark mood that Alcatraz had left within her. Lazarus held her hand easily as they went through the small shops filled with trinkets that tourists clamored for when visiting San Francisco.

"Be right back."

Lazarus left her before she could answer, and she watched him run up the wooden steps to the second floor of the Pier. Ivy was enjoying sitting in the sun watching the seals and eating her ice cream from a cup. She didn't take much time to enjoy the city that she loved but after the day she planned to not immerse herself in her art so much that she forgot the beauty around her. She already felt the inspiration to transfer her impression of the day onto the canvas.

He came back holding a small plate with a cover and held it out to her. "No ice cream is complete without two of the Crystal Sisters famous cupcakes, a staple of San Francisco and the keystone of Pier 39."

Ivy chuckled. "Were you brainwashed into being their spokesperson?"

"Hey, don't knock it, I flashed them my charm and got you an extra free cupcake," he answered.

"What else ya got there, hiding behind your back?" she asked curiously.

"This is Boo the Seal." He held out a medium sized seal wearing an Alcatraz black and white prison outfit, with big, beady eyes. "He just got out of the slammer and needs a home. He wondered if it may be with you."

"That's adorable, and he's fat, I love him," Ivy

gushed and then teased, "Are you sure he isn't your lunch?"

Lazarus grinned wickedly as he sat down and snagged a cupcake from the plate. "My wolf likes the taste of cupcakes more than seal blubber."

She wrinkled her nose at him. "Gross description."

The sun was setting by the time he took her back to her apartment. The air had taken on the chill of the breeze coming off the water, and the orange rays of lights bounced off the large glass and metal heart art installation pieces permanently secured in Union Square. Ivy had always loved them, and she kept her eyes riveted on her favorite one that featured a lighthouse and seascape painted on the front.

"Are any of them yours?" Lazarus asked.

Ivy laughed. "I was barely dreaming of being an artist when they were installed. Maybe one day they'll extend an invitation for others to be created, and I'll get a chance."

"I can make that happen if you want," Lazarus offered.

Ivy shook her head in refusal. "No thank you, if I create anything or am invited to showcase my art it will be on the merit of my work, nothing more or less."

"Understood."

In a few minutes they were outside of her apartment, and she stood awkwardly in front of him when he opened the car door for her to get out.

"Thank you for a day," she said looking up at him.

"Don't forget Bugsy the seal," he said with a smile.

"I thought his name was Boo?" She laughed.

"He looked meaner as time went by," he explained. "He's more of a Bugsy now."

"How about his name be Bugsy Boo, that way we both get what we want?"

"I know what I want," he said quietly, and with his wide hands on her shoulders he pulled her closer. "I won't give up until I have it."

A whimper barely escaped her before he took her lips in a kiss that seared her senses. Heat raced along her spine until she arched in pleasure and pressed herself more fully against him. Something inside her opened up, and she felt the primal urge to bite his lips and mark him as her own. Lazarus didn't tempt or tease his way into her mouth but speared his tongue deep, tasting and owning her lips as he devoured her with his kiss.

She vaguely heard someone clear their throat

before the husky voice said, "Lazarus, you're needed."

"Silvia, your timing is terrible," Lazarus said when he lifted his head away from hers and never looked away.

"Apparently so, but the fact remains your presence is required," Silvia said.

Lazarus growled his frustration, and Ivy didn't know why the urge to strike out at the woman became such a strong urge but when she growled in response her eyes widened in surprise. Again, she was terrified of what was going on within her, and she stepped out of his embrace quickly.

"You should go," Ivy said bluntly and grabbed the seal from the car before walking toward the apartment door.

"I get what I want, Ivy," he called after her.

"That won't be me," she yelled back without turning around.

She didn't feel safe until she was in her apartment. Ivy locked the door and pressed her back against the heavy wood as if she expected him to break the door down. *Big bad wolf,* the words raced through her brain as she walked to her bedroom. For some reason a cool shower seemed to be the only thing that would calm the raging emotions and heated blood that danced in her veins. Ivy stripped quickly and went directly to the bathroom, and after setting the water to the temperature she wanted she stepped under the spray. In true San Francisco fashion, the weather changed quickly, and when she came out of the bathroom drying her hair, the rain was beating against the windows of her apartment and running down the glass in rivulets.

Ivy dressed in a comfortable t-shirt and shorts before putting on a pair of socks. She walked to her kitchen and pulled a bottle of her favorite wine from the wine fridge and poured a glass. Ivy took the glass to the bay seat and sat down. She did what always came naturally to her when she needed to work things out in her head. Ivy covered herself with the afghan and stared out the window at the rain. Impulsively, she got up and took the stuffed seal off her bed where she had dropped him earlier. Back under the blanket she watched the lightning cut through the night sky and sipped her wine, hoping that when she looked into darkness, she would find answers to what she was feeling.

Lazarus kept his eyes on the road as the windshield wipers went furiously back and forth.

Silvia sat beside him, and he could see the headlights behind him of the car she had showed up in with Luca now in the driver's seat. She updated him as they drove, and he channeled his frustrations of being interrupted with Ivy into the situation that was developing in his district.

"I see things are going well with the Bellefonte girl," Silvia commented.

"Hardly. We run hot and cold, I don't know what works and what doesn't," Lazarus answered. "Right now, we have a lot of questions, very few answers, and apparently some baseborn activity that is either worrisome or tied to her."

"Her mutt friend practically screams it's tied to her," Silvia drawled. "Still, a good hunt in the rain always makes your mood better, and maybe we can get answers."

"Think you can keep up in stiletto heels, Sil?" Lazarus teased.

She laughed. "Please, when in all of our years have I ever been not able to catch my prey?"

"I need it alive, or at least able to answer some questions," Lazarus ordered.

"I'll be sure to tell Luca. You know his bite is way worse than his bark," Silvia reminded him. She hesitated. "Did you see her eyes when she heard my voice?"

"Yes, I did." Lazarus felt his cock ache

thinking about kissing her. "She was like fire and ice in my arms. The energy rolling off her was incredible."

"She's the one then, even if she doesn't know who or what she really is," Silvia assessed.

"Ivy is more than I ever dreamed of but this must be handled carefully." Lazarus sighed in frustration. "Claiming her is all I want but so much has been hidden from her that when it all comes out, she may run. Then she will be the most coveted prize."

"Don't worry boss, you'll be the one," Silvia assured him.

Lazarus grunted and focused on the road. He wanted Ivy in the worst way. She was truly magnificent and he would kill all who stepped in his path. Even the baseborn friend whose agenda Lazarus had yet to figure out.

Chapter Four

Two days later, Ivy pulled up outside of her agent's office. Bunny's office was located in one of the newer Pac buildings that intersected on Soma and the busy San Francisco financial district. She parked the car and fed the meter a few extra quarters knowing how much Bunny could talk, especially when she was excited. This was finally payday from the gallery opening a few weeks ago, and depending on the size of her check Ivy was considering a vacation and shopping in New York to get away for at least a week or two before her next big project. Ivy took a minute and looked at the high rises, marveling at her hometown and the blue sky. She wondered if Lazarus had offices uptown.

Of course he does, dolt. He is the alpha, and the financial district was his bread and butter, the hub of everything. He wouldn't be the mogul he is without lording down on everyone from high above, she thought.

She felt bad about her internal dialogue because they left on good terms Saturday when he dropped her off. Granted, she hadn't heard from him since, and that was two days ago, but what did she expect. She grimaced in frustration. She didn't want to marry him, and yet there she was wondering why he hadn't called. *You have issues, Ivy Bellefonte*, she told herself as she walked into the office building. *Serious issues that may need to be discussed in therapy.*

Bunny's receptionist looked up with a smile when she walked in. "Go right in, Ivy, she is expecting you."

"Thanks Jacqueline." Ivy returned the smile. "Any day now, huh?"

Jacqueline rubbed her round belly and sighed. "I hope so, because this kid is playing kickball with my bladder."

"Good luck, and shoot me a text when he finally makes his debut. I want to send you a gift basket," Ivy said. "I don't know what Bunny is going to do without you while you are on maternity leave."

"My sister takes over working in my place for the time, and since we're twins, it will be like I'm here," Jacqueline explained and winked. "Plus, I'll be on speed dial when it comes to Bunny's, to put it mildly, quirks."

Ivy laughed. "Yep, she certainly doesn't deal with change well."

When she opened the door to the office, Bunny was talking on the phone. She wiggled slender fingers at Ivy and waved at her to sit down. Ivy studied her surroundings as Bunny yelled into the phone.

"Armando, I don't care if your muses flew away like *One Flew Over The Cuckoo's Nest*," Bunny yelled into the phone. "This gallery opening is one of the most important of your life, and I practically bled to make it happen. Do you want to see my fingers from dialing the phone and my lips from kissing ass? They are sore, Armando, both of them, so kick your muses in the ass and get the pieces done. They're going in the gallery even if the paint is dripping wet."

Ivy listened silently, knowing that once or twice she had been on the receiving end of one of those calls. Bunny was a formidable woman and barely five feet tall. Ivy very much believed that if she was put in the ring with a boxer, she would go spider monkey on her opponent and they would be doomed.

"Ivy, earth to Ivy," Bunny snapped her fingers. "Focus on me, darling. I am about to blow your mind."

"You have my full attention, Bunny," Ivy said.

"Does that mean my check is good enough for my New York trip?"

Bunny laughed and handed her a check. "Several trips, darling, every piece sold."

"You're kidding... that's wonderful!" Ivy gasped in delight and looked at the paper in her hand. The zeros behind the main number was quite impressive. "I'll take two weeks, and I'll be working diligently to get ready for the fall show."

"I'm glad to hear it but you won't because I will no longer be your agent," Bunny said with a devious smile.

"You're dropping me?" Ivy asked in alarm. "Bunny, I won't take the trip if necessary. You are the most amazing agent I ever had. If this is my check, I'm sure you made just as much if not more..."

"Ivy, calm yourself. You know my Zen gets ruined in charged emotional situations," Bunny held up her hands. "I won't be your agent anymore because our contract has been bought out."

"What, by who?" Ivy asked.

"Lazarus Vale," Bunny said and handed her a manila envelope.

Ivy felt like cold water had been thrown over her. Lazarus meant that every move she made was to be dictated by him one way or another, regardless of what she wanted or how she felt.

"I won't accept that," Ivy said stubbornly. "I signed with you, and first, he isn't even an art agent. Second, that would be a breach of contract or something."

Bunny shook her head slowly. "Sweetie, you read the clause where I, as your agent, can sell your contract to another party for the term of the contract. Which means that for the next two years he is your agent."

"No, I'll fight this in court." Ivy felt like crying; in fact, tears burned her eyes. "Please don't do this to me, Bunny."

Bunny looked at her sympathetically. "Ivy Bellefonte, when have I ever done anything that wasn't in your best interest? You have the potential to reach the top of the art world and take it by storm. My way could take years, with the Vale name behind you, your art will be coveted."

"I don't want the Vale name behind me, I want this in my way," Ivy cried out. "That man just wants to own me like he does everything else in this damn town, and I'm sick of it."

"The deal is done, Ivy," Bunny said firmly. "Put on your big girl panties and deal with it. You know this is a business and your livelihood. Don't be a silly girl, be a woman and do yourself proud. It's your art that you are selling, not his name."

"Is that all?" Ivy said stiffly.

"Yes, and congratulations even if you don't see it now." Bunny smiled. "I look forward to seeing your show in the fall."

Without another word, Ivy took her check and left Bunny's office. She nodded at Jacqueline, who gave her a sad smile as she stormed out of the door. The check in her hand would be last that she could really call her own, because now she wouldn't know if she if they truly liked her work or if it was because of Lazarus's name. In her car, she took pictures of the contract and sent them via email before she called Trent. He would have answers—he was a lawyer, after all.

"Hey lady, please tell me you are calling me to go to lunch and escape the doldrums that is my life." Owen's voice was pleasant.

"I just left Bunny's office, where she told me that Lazarus bought out my contract," Ivy said. "I sent pictures to your email. I need you to check it over for me."

"Holy shit," Trent gasped. "Yeah, one second, opening my email now... but Ivy, I'm just a small time litigator..."

"I don't have the energy to boost your ego and tell you how great you are, please just look." She sighed.

"Oh honey, this is some high-class legal jargon." Trent gave a low whistle after a few minutes. "It's airtight. Lazarus probably had a team of lawyers draw up this fucking thing because it is like the super mega cyborg of contracts."

"That's just fucking great," Ivy muttered.

"Calm down, drive over to my office, and we'll talk about it," Trent suggested.

"Exactly what will that do?" Ivy asked in frustration and sighed. "Sorry, Trent, I don't mean to take this out on you."

"I know. Where are you heading?" Trent asked.

"To the bank and then to pay for my dad and brother's rent," Ivy said. "I'll give you a call later, thanks for checking."

She stopped at the bank and took out enough cash to pay the rest and her father and brother's bills. They usually spent what they made at the docks on themselves, knowing she would take care of everything else. This was the last time, she promised herself. Apparently, she could only depend on herself. She drove to the small trailer park where they lived and parked beside a new truck and a compact car. Their red pickup truck was gone, and she had no doubt who was behind the new wheels. She climbed the rickety, creaking wooden steps and opened the semi rusted screen door. Inside, boxes were everywhere.

"Dad, Eric?"

Eric came out of the kitchen with food in his mouth, as he always did. With the way he ate she wondered why he wasn't bigger instead of his beanpole frame. Her father came out of the bedroom holding a handful of shirts.

"Hi babygirl," her father said warmly. "I didn't expect to see you today."

"I came to pay the rent and the bills," Ivy said. "Probably take you guys shopping for food. What's going on with the new wheels and the packing?"

"Sis, you know." Eric grinned. "Your impending marriage has moved us up in status. No need to pay for nothing, we're good."

"I'm not marrying Lazarus Vale so you may want to rethink the move," she snapped and turned to her father. "He bought out my contract, Dad. He threw a shitload of money toward Bunny and now he owns me, and you apparently have no problem with that."

Her father put the shirts in his old recliner and moved toward her. He cupped her cheek and looked down at her lovingly. "Ivy, I want you to be protected, more than I ever could. There are things out there…"

"What things, Dad?" she cried out. "Are cars and a new place to live worth my happiness, my life? Hell, take my whole fucking check and do what you want but at least be on my side."

"Ivy, you trust me, *wi*? You need to have a strong man to keep you safe."

"Like that baseborn could do anything," Eric snorted.

"For a man who lives off his sister you're a fine one to talk." Ivy glared at her brother.

"Hey, we're family," Eric protested.

"Just grow the fuck up and act your age, Eric. You're a man, not a teenager always stuffing your face and being a complete asshole!" Ivy yelled. "For Christ's sake, from the time I was old enough to reach the stove I was cooking for you two, cleaning up after you, couldn't date because dinner needed to be on the table. Reminding you, Dad, to give me the money for bills and rent. Food shopping, laundry..." Ivy swiped the hot tears that streaked down her face. "All I asked is that you both defend me, be there for me, not be selfish as you usually are. Well I'm done. Take Lazarus's money but be ready for him to own you because I will never marry him. Work it off being the pets to his pack for all I care."

"Ivy..." her father pleaded, and she saw tears in his eyes.

"Oh, here's my contribution to your new life. Like I said, it's the last time."

Her father held out his arms for her, and for a moment, she was tempted to run to him for the comfort. She used to rub her nose against his scratchy shirt when she was a child, and he would sit in his beat up recliner and tell her stories of princesses and castles in the sand. Somewhere along the line she became their caretaker, not a daughter or a sister, and it was time for that to end.

She shook her head furiously and threw one last angry glare at her brother who looked at her with sullen eyes before she walked out the door. Ivy started the car and wanted to go home and cry, but she refused to shed any more tears. What was it with the men in her life? This was a time when she longed for her mother but she could barely remember the bright smile and the laugh that seemed to be only an echo in her dreams. Sometimes she could recall the blue of her eyes set into a soft brown face, or the smell of a floral perfume reminded her of the woman she barely knew.

Ivy was sure if her mother was still alive, she would have been someone who stood with her, but instead she felt even more alone. Ivy firmed her shoulders and did what most people in her situation wouldn't do. It felt like she drove around for hours until the sun started to set. Ivy made her decision and turned her car toward what she and Trent called the ivory tower and headed into the wolf's den.

Chapter Five

Lazarus knew she was at his door before the doorbell rang. He scented her, wanted her, and the animal within him longed for her. He also knew that she was mad because even behind the barrier her scent was more intoxicating. Angry, sweaty, hot sex would suit his mood right now but she was here and upset. That meant she had talked with Bunny. He was alone at home because this was his private sanctuary but usually there were at least three of his people with him at all times.

Luca, Silvia, and one of the others were running down leads. Deception was at play, and the pieces were in motion. Ivy was at the center and must be protected at all cost. He opened the door, and she stood there seething, her pink sundress against creamy dark skin and her face framed against the last of the sunset casting a halo around her head. It made her look absolutely scrumptious. She glared at him, shooting daggers with her eyes. Lazarus leaned against the door casually and assessed her. *I wonder how mad I'd have to make her…* He let the thought slide away as his arousal heightened.

"Ivy, I never thought you'd grace my doorstep… Willingly," he drawled.

She slapped the contract against his chest and pushed past him. "Please, you knew I would show up here."

"Well yes, after asking your little baseborn friend to read the contract, then go to your father's house for moral support." Lazarus closed the door. "You're ahead of schedule. I was expecting you to rain down wrath upon my head tomorrow."

"Sure, because ruining my life is funny to you," Ivy said and stopped in the foyer and looked around. "Where's the alcohol in this place?"

"Through that door." He pointed and tried to hide his amusement as he followed her. "Are we sharing a drink?"

"We should celebrate the fact that you have integrated yourself in every facet of my fucking life." Ivy walked to the bar and picked up a decanter.

Lazarus watched as she poured a healthy portion into a glass and took a gulp, and her eyes began to water.

"Maybe you'd like some wine instead," he offered.

"No, I'll drink your expensive whiskey," she managed to choke out.

"Then I'll have one with you, since we're celebrating and all." Lazarus moved toward the bar, and she took her glass and made sure to move away from him.

"Why are you using me as some sort of amusement for Lazarus Vale?" Ivy asked. "Truly, I want to know. It's like a cat playing with a mouse, or a wolf playing with a rabbit."

"It may seem that way but I honestly care about your well-being," Lazarus said gently. It was more than that, so much more, but he couldn't tell her—not yet.

She laughed sarcastically. "Yes, because buying a marriage to me and my contract from my agent shows caring. You don't want me, you deserve someone like that woman who's always trailing behind you."

"Silvia?" Lazarus laughed out loud. "She's like my sister, and she likes knives way too much. I think she sleeps with daggers under her pillow."

She took another small sip of her drink and grimaced. "Really then... Oh, she's like protection."

"I don't need to be protected, but as Alpha I

have those who I trust above all others. Silvia and her brother Luca are two of those people," Lazarus explained. "Still, because of my standing many would like to see me fall. The treaty between clans is very fragile and to see me dead could cause an all out war."

She raised an elegant eyebrow at him. "So... protection."

He nodded with a smile. "A little, yes."

"Back to why I'm such an interesting commodity to you and how the hell do I get out of it," Ivy said.

"You're not a hostage, Ivy. I want to make your life better," Lazarus said. "Marrying me would enhance your status and your career."

She slammed the glass down on the mantle. "Why do you think my life is so bad? I can make it on my own and was doing very well until you showed up at my gallery opening. I don't need or want your status."

"You need my status, trust me," Lazarus replied.

"For Christ's sake, why?" Ivy asked in exasperation. "I'm a human in your world, I am a threat to none of the clans or their districts. Telling me my life will be better with you is like Eric telling me licorice tasted good, and I didn't like that either."

Lazarus opened his mouth to answer and just as he did the ground shook. Was it a sign that she wasn't ready to know? But as his house shook, he knew it was an inopportune earthquake. A glass figurine fell off the mantle and shattered, and Ivy jumped back with a small cry.

"Doorway, now," he ordered and grabbed her hand.

Lazarus pressed her against the doorway and protectively held his body against hers as the earth moved. If anything fell and hit him, he could take it—up to an extent—but her fragile body could be crushed. The lights flickered and went dark, and he continued to hold her tight.

"Um, Lazarus, it stopped," she said against his chest. "You can move now."

He couldn't because something else was placing them in danger. He heard them outside, sulking around in the darkness. His power out meant the security was down around his house, and the gates had been breached. For the past few nights they stayed away, the lights and the high walls giving them a disadvantage. From the first night Silvia called him when he was at Ivy's loft, they figured out chimera was testing the house's security.

Someone was always there, and they'd never

take a risk with a group of wolves on the premises but an earthquake and power outage gave them a definite advantage. Just as he could scent them, they knew by now he was alone or only with a human. It didn't bode well for them in any case, because to protect what was his Lazarus was a very dangerous man indeed.

"Lazarus?"

"Shhh," he said against her ear. "Four outside, and they're going to come into the house. I want you safe before I go on the defensive."

"Who's outside, rival wolves?" she whispered, and he heard the fear in her voice.

He took her hand and led her back into the room. With a quick press against the wall a panel slid open to reveal a code box. Lazarus put the numbers in quickly, and the bookcase opened away from the wall.

"You have a panic room?" Ivy asked in disbelief.

"It came with the house," Lazarus said and pressed a hard kiss on her mouth. "If you don't see me on that monitor in thirty minutes or less, use the phone inside and press the pound button. My people will be here soon, and they will protect you. They have their orders."

"Christ, you're talking like you will be killed…"

Breaking glass cut off her words, and Lazarus pushed her inside without another word. He turned, knowing they had come in at the back side of the house, and growled deep in his throat. Lazarus gave his second nature free rein, and as the heat of his shift ran along his skin, he heard the tearing of his clothes as his body changed shape and form. He had learned long ago that as long as you give yourself over to the shift, it never hurt. As his face elongated to a snout and his body went down to all fours, Lazarus howled to let them know he was coming. They wouldn't survive the night.

He bounded out of the room and could hear his sharp claws against the tile. The crashing sound in the kitchen drew his attention, and he ran down the hall. Drawing them outside to chase him wasn't an option because as soon as he entered the room, two jumped on him from each side. Sharp teeth tried to sink into the flesh of his neck and side but because of his thick fur it was barely a scrape. He shook them off easily, and a primal snarl left his mouth as he charged the one in front and caught it around the neck.

Lazarus's wolf bit down until he felt bone shatter beneath his teeth, and with a vicious whip of his neck he heard the bone snap. He let out a howl of anger as one of the baseborn attackers bit his hind leg, hoping to stop him while the other two attacked. Lazarus shook his leg free, and they attacked with furious, destructive intent. He ripped the throat from one more, reveling in the taste of its blood. and It shuddered on the tile floor as it bled out. The other two seemed to rethink attacking, but it was already too late — they were not leaving alive. The third baseborn ran, and he pounced on the mangy body, his weight stopping its escape.

The fourth tried to help its friend and jumped on Lazarus's back but failed to get its smaller mouth around his neck. Lazarus barely felt the pain from the bite. Instead, he stepped on the third baseborn's neck until its struggling ceased and then proceeded to rip the last one apart. In the middle of the mayhem and destruction he let out a howl of victory.

He tried to take control but his savage wolf was unwilling to let go. The wolf was free and wanted to run, to find more of their enemies and feel the life drain out of them under its massive bite. *Water.* The word filtered into his mind as he struggled to regain the upper hand. It had never been like this before, he could always shift back to human form easily. But this time Ivy was there, and his second nature wanted to protect its mate so the internal battle had begun.

Lazarus propelled his wolf body outside and using the need to quench its thirst he went to the pool. The wolf wanted to drink but as the two sides struggled for control of the body they shared, he threw himself into the water. The hope that the cold liquid would shock his wolf into obeying proved futile. In minutes, he was out, shaking his fur to get rid of excess droplets before stalking back inside. He looked at the carnage with satisfaction and followed the scent of his mate in the house. Lazarus put his forepaws on the bookcase and scraped at it, trying to get in to see Ivy. All he wanted—needed—was her, and his wolf was incensed at the barrier. In a howl of rage, he destroyed furniture and paced the room. His human side knew that the wolf would not acquiesce control without seeing her, so it waited and raged.

"Lazarus…"

He heard his name and turned to stare as she slipped from behind the bookcase. A low growl escaped him and stopped her in her steps. He stood back and so did she. He watched as Ivy got to her knees and put her hand on the soft rug in front of her.

"Lazarus, it's all good now, we are safe. You can rest." She rubbed the carpet in front of her in a repetitive motion, and his eyes followed her hands. "Come over here and lie down, please. It's okay, we are both safe."

He moved forward slowly and lay down on the carpet in front of her before placing his snout on her hands.

"There you go. You're so tired, I heard you protecting me, saw the monitors in the kitchen," Ivy talked as she ran her hand along his damp fur. "I was scared, but you protected me like you said you would."

Her comforting tone soothed the beast within him and slowly he felt his wolf give up the fight within and Lazarus was able to take his body back.

"You're bleeding," she gasped and touched his side when he was in human form.

"It's already healing," his voice was a rasp, and he looked at her with hungry eyes. He moved toward her stealthily on his hands and knees like the predator wolf who lived within him. She moved back, and it was like a slow motion burlesque dance as he covered her body with his own naked one. He nuzzled her neck, and she gasped. Lazarus looked at her. "Accept me."

"I don't know what you what me to say," Ivy said timidly.

He took her hand and wrapped it around his

engorged cock, growling as he felt her touch. "Accept me, be mine, take me inside you, mate with me."

He closed his eyes and arched into her touch as she stroked his length.

"Yes."

At her simple answer, he kissed her with a grunt of satisfaction. His hands weren't gentle. He knew he should try as he tore at her blouse and felt the soft material give under his hands. The bra didn't stand a chance as he kissed his way down to her chest and sucked on her nipples hungrily. Her soft cry fueled his need, and the wolf within drove him to take her in the most primal and carnal way.

He moved his open mouth down to her torso, tasting her skin and loving her scent as he tried to open the button of her linen slacks. He lost his patience with the button in seconds, grabbing both sides and tearing it open. The zip and the button gave way, and he dragged the pants down her legs, taking the white lace panties with them.

He looked up at Ivy and loved how her kiss swollen lips were parted with anticipation. He buried his face between her legs and lapped at the soft flesh of her pussy greedily. God, her musk and her scent drove him mad. His wolf was pleased, so very pleased, with everything about her. It only made him more primal in his human form to claim her as his. Lazarus delved his tongue deeper between the moist folds, and her cry of desire and the way her body gave up its essence against his tongue filled him with a sense of satisfaction.

"Lazarus, oh my god, what... Oh, I can't believe..."

He groaned in pleasure. She couldn't even form a thought under his mouth. He fucked with his tongue, grabbing her hips and pulling her against his tongue as he speared it inside her. Ivy's release was hard, and her body shook under his ministrations. He lifted his head and looked at her with her hands gripping the carpet and the rise and fall of her chest.

"That's what I wanted, to see you come and know it's me who made you feel that way." Lazarus's voice was harsh with desire as he spoke.

He flipped her over so she was on her stomach and raised her onto her knees. Ivy was bent at the elbows looking back at him with a look of wanton need, and he licked him lips in anticipation. Lazarus rubbed the head of his cock along the slit of her sex and watched it glisten with a coating of her juices. He slipped into her slowly, knowing that he was engorged, rock hard, and bigger than most normal human men.

He didn't even want to think about anyone who may have touched her; it made him want to find them all and rip them apart. *Mine*, he thought, and with a final short thrust he was buried all the way into her wet depths. He loved the sensation of her pussy wrapped around his cock, the walls of her sex clenched at him greedily. He threw his head back, his neck taut as he held onto her hips, striving for control.

"Move, Lazarus, please… God I need to feel you," Ivy moaned breathlessly.

"Yes."

The word escaped him in a guttural whisper. He pulled out slowly and sank himself within her once more. It was like every nerve ending could feel her glide along his cock.

"Deeper, harder," she begged on a moan.

"Yes, love," Lazarus muttered.

He began pounding into her, harder with each thrust, until she screamed his name in pleasure. Ivy was on her hands and knees now, pushing back against his cock and taking every inch of him. She pleased him so much; her response to him was more than he thought possible. Ivy arched like a sleek cat, the lines of her curvaceous body like the art she created. He bent over and ran his tongue down the line of her back, tasting the sheen of sweat that had formed on her skin.

"I'm going to come, Lazarus," Ivy said on a keening cry.

Lazarus fucked her from behind and pulled her up so she was on her knees in front of him. His hand was on her neck and he turned her face to him as he drove himself into her with wild abandon. She moaned as he devoured her mouth and Lazarus felt her release shake her at the core. The gush of slick fluid that ran down around his cock allowed him to glide deeper. The way the walls of her sex clung to him drove him mad as if she was not willing to give up the pleasure they both were immersed in.

He closed his eyes and gave himself over to his own orgasm. His balls tightened and his cock throbbed as he spilled his hot seed inside her. He pumped into her repeatedly until they fell, pliant against the carpet, and the only thing that could be heard was their breathing in the empty room. He felt a sense of completion as Ivy lay cocooned against him after their mating. He nuzzled her neck, and she laughed and ran her nails along his back. Lazarus shuddered and arched against her.

"You like that?" she said.

"It sounds wolf cliché, I know, but I love my back being scratched," he admitted.

Just then they heard the sound of splintered wood and someone yelled "Lazarus!" He looked at her and pulled a soft cashmere blanket off the nearby chair to cover them.

"I kinda forgot I pressed the panic button when you took too long to come back," Ivy admitted and buried her face into his arm as his pack rushed into the living room.

"Well, he looks more than fine," Silvia drawled. She'd rushed in along with Luca who had a grin on his face and two others of his pack who looked like they were ready to take on whatever fight had gone on in his house.

"The mess is in the kitchen," Lazarus said. "Let me get Ivy upstairs and I'll come down."

"Take your time boss," Luca said. His accent was slight but still very noticeable. "We should keep any who are outside from coming in here before the scent drives them into a mating frenzy."

"You are a barrel of laughs," Lazarus said casually.

"Baseborn?" Silvia asked.

"Yes, they were skulking around outside as usual but the earthquake knocked the power and the security grid out." Lazarus stood unashamed of his nakedness and wrapped Ivy in the blanket. She was so embarrassed her entire body was covered in a heat, and damn if he didn't want to kiss every inch of her skin once more. "I killed all four in the kitchen."

"Five. There were tracks outside," Silvia said. "You only sensed four?"

"I was worried about... other things," Lazarus admitted. In the back of his mind he wondered what would happen if they had killed him and managed to get to Ivy. It was one of the reasons his shift was so difficult to return to, the wolf within him wanted to protect her at all costs.

"We can see that." Silvia looked directly at Ivy as she spoke and then turned to head toward the kitchen. "We'll be starting the clean up of the incident in the kitchen."

Lazarus lifted her into his arms. "Let's get you to my bed."

"Lazarus, I'm embarrassed enough, at least let me walk," she protested.

He kissed her temple. "You have nothing to be ashamed of, you had delicious sex with your mate in his home." He growled in her ear. "You smell delectable, and I plan to taste you a few more times before the night is done."

"We are not mated," she protested. "We had sex like two consenting adults, nothing more."

"You say potato, I say..."

"Potato, because you are going to give me

time to make my own choices," she finished for him.

"Maybe," he said noncommittally.

He reached down while still holding her and opened the door to his master bedroom. Nothing gave Lazarus more satisfaction than placing his mate on the king size bed that sat in the center of the room. Ivy's wild, dark brown hair was spread out on his pillow, the bronze expanse of skin a contrast against the gray sheets. He wanted to climb into bed and share an intimate kiss before immersing himself in the dilatable nectar that was Ivy.

He was warm natured and kept the room cool, Lazarus watched as she shivered before he pulled his thick down comforter over Ivy's nakedness for added warmth. Later, he would pull her close, snuggled against the heat of his skin, protecting her as he was meant to do. He sat on the side of the bed and watched as she blinked sleepily. A combination of the alcohol she wasn't accustomed to, the fear, and their loving probably took more energy than she realized.

"Sleep." He kissed her. "I'll be back soon. You are safe here, trust me."

"I know," she whispered and snuggled down into the bed.

He watched her drift off before going to the

closet and pulling out a pair of sweat pants. Wearing only that and barefoot, he headed back downstairs to his pack. *There were five,* he repeated the words in his head grimly. This was a planned attack, and the small earthquake had given them an advantage that may have taken weeks for them to find. Now it was his turn. They would find out exactly what the end game was and there would be worse than hell to pay. The culprit would answer to him.

Chapter Six

The instinct to protect her was so strong it took everything for him to leave her in his bedroom even though she was behind the door. More of his pack had shown up, and while they removed the bodies from the kitchen, Luca had left to follow the scent of the fifth baseborn he'd missed. Inside, he and Silvia did their own search in his house.

"They were after something in here, and they were willing to lose four of their people to do it," Silvia said grimly. "Tell me you don't have piles of cash in the safe."

"Please give me some credit, Sil," Lazarus said mildly. "If money was their motivation, they could have robbed the docks, or even better, the restaurant districts. They were after something specific."

Silvia inhaled deeply. "The mutt scent is very faint here, more like really bad cologne and cheap soap."

"This one didn't shift, human form," Lazarus murmured.

He moved to the large painting on the wall behind his desk. It looked like it hadn't been moved but Lazarus knew better. He could scent a trace of the baseborn's touch, and it didn't want anyone to know it was in there because his office was immaculate compared to the destruction in his kitchen. Lazarus knew what he kept there, and he was sure it was gone by now. He took the painting off the wall and looked at the open compartment.

"Is it secure? I know Ricky and Collin put it in top notch systems," Silvia said as she moved forward.

"Earthquake knocked out the system, and we haven't set up the secondary power grid yet," Lazarus replied. "I was lucky the damn panic room has its own power source."

"Boss, you bought the place eight months ago…" Silvia said.

Lazarus looked at her and irritation boiled within him. He pushed it back, knowing that she was only looking out for her Alpha. "I know this, since I signed the papers. But the business, the pack, comes first. They were going to install when we had a lull in system orders."

"Understood." She didn't smile but gave him a raised eyebrow.

Silvia was as cool as they came, and she was

the best of his enforcers. Sometimes he wondered if she feared him, and other times he doubted she was afraid of anything. She never showed any interest in mating or having children. Lazarus had seen her shoot down other males in the pack with a simple "no." They didn't dare push the issue.

"They took the files and the book," Lazarus said after searching the safe.

"So it is about her and who she is," Silvia confirmed. "You're going to have to seal this mating sooner rather than later, boss, to protect your interest in this."

"It's to protect her," Lazarus said. "When I found out... the entire story, it is imperative that her safety is one hundred percent the mission, at all costs."

"Her mutt friend may have some stake in this. Should we sit on him and see where he goes?" Silvia asked.

"Yes, and keep a very good stance away. I think this is bigger than him and bigger than any of us realize," Lazarus said. "Imagine the implications of what they could be planning if they know who she is."

"We should just align with the other districts and wipe them off the face of the earth," Silvia snarled.

"I won't condone or give approval for mass genocide of a people," Lazarus said. "We will handle this quietly, root out the offenders, and deal with them in kind. When I am not with her, I need two people watching her at all times. If there is any trouble they are allowed to kill on sight and get her to safety."

Silvia nodded. "Yes to that boss. Would you prefer me to be the one to watch her?"

Lazarus shook his head. "I need my best enforcer on the hunt. Have Andy and Mikal watch her when she leaves here."

"Planning on a long weekend?" Silvia teased.

Lazarus smiled. "You never know. How is my kitchen looking?"

"It's almost back to pristine condition," she answered. "We'll get done and leave, and we'll keep you updated on progress. I think you should probably tell her, Lazarus. Until she knows who she truly is, she won't ever be able to protect herself. What if we aren't there? She should know."

Lazarus sighed and dragged his hand through his hair. "It's not my truth to tell, Sil. I can talk to those involved and see, but in the end, learning the truth from me may drive her further away."

"If you say so." Silvia left the office without another word.

Silvia would never push the issue with him, but Lazarus could hear the doubt in her voice. She thought he was wrong. Maybe he was, but Lazarus had to let this play out the way his instincts dictated. After he made sure his office wasn't missing anything else, he went into the kitchen and true to word it looked like it did before.

He knew his pack would discreetly take care of the bodies, and from there, carry out his orders. There would be much discussion at the next pack meeting, and he was sure there would be talk of war with the baseborns for this attack. Hopefully before then he'd have the situation with Ivy remedied. Then he could focus on the reins he kept tightly held to keep the districts from all-out war.

Two of his pack stayed outside and would sleep in the guesthouse. He wasn't sleepy but the urge to have Ivy nestled in his arms was just as good as sex. In bed, she turned to him with a soft murmur, and the wolf within practically growled in pleasure. She fought so hard while she was awake, but in her dream, she gave over to the truth: she wanted to be with him. Lazarus knew that she wouldn't give up the fight so easily so for now he enjoyed her supple body against his.

"I have no clean clothes," Ivy protested.

"You look cute in my shirt," Lazarus replied as he stirred eggs in the cast iron skillet.

The kitchen was immaculate after last night's attack, and he was impressed by his people's ability to work quickly and quietly. Their night of passionate love had left him starved and feeling like he could conquer the world. Since he'd already done the world domination thing, he decided food was on the agenda. He had maple bacon in the broiler and was preparing the eggs, the coffee was on, and he had thick, sliced bread crisping in the oven.

Ivy offered to help, but Lazarus insisted she sit patiently and wait. As her mate he wanted to provide for her and make sure she was fed. He chuckled to himself, knowing if he was like that now, the day she got pregnant he would drive her crazy. He recalled how his father was when his mother was pregnant with his younger brother; she actually left and stayed in a hotel for a week to get away from him. That frazzled his father even more, and when she came home, he barely let her walk to the bathroom alone.

"What's so funny?" Ivy asked from where she sat.

"Nothing, internal joke," Lazarus answered. He transferred the eggs to one large plate. "If you're so worried about clothes, I'm sure Silvia may have something in one of the guest bedrooms."

Ivy laughed. "I don't think anything the glamazon wears would fit me without hanging off my arms and legs. Are you sure you guys aren't, you know… friends with benefits?"

Lazarus laughed out loud. "Please no, since she works for me and is one of my closest confidants in the pack. She stays here occasionally, as well as many of my pack at some point or the other."

"Where do they all live?" Ivy asked.

Lazarus piled bacon and bread on the plate before pouring the coffee and sitting across from her. "They all have their own places. We have a compound outside the city for pack meetings."

"Good to know." She looked around. "I see my coffee but where's my plate and fork?"

"We just need one," Lazarus said. "I'll feed you."

"I can feed myself," she pointed out. He smiled and held a fork full of the fluffy eggs to her lips. "I'm aware, but I want to do this. Open up for me, sweetheart."

She did as he asked and after chewing gave

him a curious look. "Is this a wolf thing? I feel like this one of the things that as a human I wouldn't understand."

If you only knew, he thought but nodded. "Yes, I'm caring for my mate."

"What if I'm not your mate, and this is just great sex?" Ivy asked. She chewed the half slice of bacon he held to her lips.

"It's something we instinctively know, and trust me, I know," he answered.

"For humans it doesn't work that way, Lazarus," she said gently. "I need to know you and love you before I can commit to us and a life together."

"And can you?" He looked at her directly. "Love me, I mean?"

"I don't know," she admitted.

"Is it because I am the Lord and master, the myth, the legend, and one may have to bow and scrape in my presence?" Lazarus asked.

She gasped and slapped at his hand. "I knew you heard us, I knew it!"

"Wolves have impeccable hearing." He took a bite of their large breakfast. "Plus your mutt…"

"Trent," she corrected him.

He sighed dramatically. "Trent was loud enough to raise the dead. You'd think as baseborn he would know that we can hear quite well."

"In his defense, Trent doesn't like to shift. He said it feels uncomfortable, and he's above that," Ivy said.

Lazarus made a sound of disgust in the back of his throat. "Even as a baseborn, he shouldn't turn his back on his second nature. He's weak."

"He wants more than is provided for baseborns," Ivy said, and he saw the defiance in her eyes. "They get scraps of work, food, finances, and well, everything from the other districts. I don't understand when the treaty was made why they weren't offered more of an alternative for their people to survive."

"I'll tell you a story," Lazarus said as he fed her. "Once upon a time, the wolf packs of San Francisco waged a bloody war against each other. Losses on each side were monumental, all fighting to be at the top of the ladder. Baseborns fought for who could pay them the most, and finally, when the Alpha's of each pack decided to finally end the fighting and form a treaty, dividing the world unseen by humans in the city, the baseborns were offered a stake in the treaty."

"They were part of it all from the beginning?" Ivy asked.

Lazarus nodded. "Very much so because textiles are a big commodity in this city, and they were to have that district. But the Alpha of the baseborns was greedy; more profit could be made if the fighting continued, and the loss of his people were acceptable as long as the money came in."

"That's terrible," Ivy breathed.

"It was, and it became worse at the final treaty meeting where the Alpha's of each pack were to sign in blood and forge the lines of each district," Lazarus explained. "The baseborn leader attacked the meeting, and his people were directed to blame the other pack leaders so they wouldn't trust each other. The attack came from all sides, with each baseborn who lead in the killing claiming one of the wolves Alphas ordered it. My father was attacked the worst because he was the leader of all the wolves."

"I don't get that—if each pack has an Alpha, how do you and your family end up at the top of the food chain?" Ivy questioned.

"Hush, my darling, let me finish my story. I'll get to that." Lazarus winked at her and fed her a piece of bread. "There was one baseborn who wasn't willing to die for their leader's ultimate plan. To save his life when caught, he revealed the plan. Because of this, the baseborn was banished to lower districts and textiles was encompassed into the manufacturing districts. The baseborns would work and survive without any pack's help."

"Because of one man's actions, the entire baseborn pack was punished?" Ivy frowned. "That seems unfair."

"That's life in this world. If I were to fall, my pack would be left defenseless," Lazarus explained. "They would have to be encompassed by another pack or females used for mating. While all the males would have to beg to be let into the clan starting at the lowest ranks, wolves need a pack. A lone wolf would go insane and attack human or wolf alike. To be lone wolves—which is just as bad—either way, death would be the only solution."

"Christ almighty, that is harsh," Ivy breathed. "Being human is simpler."

"Not really, it's a more vicious cycle because people tend to look out for themselves. We look out for our pack, and every decision is based on that," Lazarus answered.

"Which leads back to the original question: why is the Vale pack at the top of the food chain?" Ivy asked.

"Because of our bloodline. I am an alpha whose leadership comes from not only strength but within," Lazarus explained.

"That doesn't tell me a darn thing," Ivy replied.

"Okay, think about a Vulcan mind meld."

Lazarus laughed at her expression. "Because of my family's bloodline even other Alphas must submit to me. I was born into it but it could have just as easily been Kristoff's pack or any of the others. We had the money and the power to lead them all. My ancestors took the financial district because we are the largest piece of the machine. Nothing can happen without banking, stocks, bonds, and the like."

"Money is power, and your people made sure they wielded it all," Ivy murmured.

"In essence, yes." Lazarus could feel the reservations rolling off her in waves. "Ivy, I am fair, I'm honest, I don't take what is not ours, I don't cheat, and I don't take my responsibilities lightly."

"But if someone crossed you, you could cripple their business and ruin their lives," she surmised.

He met her gaze. "Yes, I can, but it's not something I would do unless truly warranted. I want everyone to be happy and survive, and because of this, I will look into the baseborn's lives and see if I can ease restrictions in some way."

"You'd do that because of me?" Ivy asked surprised.

"There is almost nothing I wouldn't do to

make you smile." Lazarus lifted her fingertips to his lips and kissed them.

"You're really good at this charm and courting thing," she said, and he felt her pulse speed up.

It was a surprise that he wanted her again, to take her and fuck her until they were sweaty and pliant between rumpled sheets. But after last night, he knew that she would need some time because in some instances he was rough, and she had to be tender or slightly sore between her legs. But he knew they couldn't stay inside all day, if not, he would surely have her in his bed, and each time the need to take her hit him, she would be naked and wet when he touched her.

"Let's go to San Diego for the day," Lazarus said, offering a solution to take his mind off her naked body.

"That's impromptu. We'd have to go by my place so I can grab something to wear," she said with a smile. "I like this impulsive nature you seem to possess."

"Call me Mr. Spontaneity," he said. "Besides, the private jet is at our personal air strip, and it's an easy call to the pilot."

"At least you didn't say you could fly us yourself," Ivy teased.

"You wouldn't trust me to pilot you anywhere you wanted to go?"

Ivy winked, and she took up a piece of bacon and held it to his lips instead of the other way around. "I trust you to take me to the stars but in other ways."

"You naughty minx, don't tease the wolf because he may want to gobble you up again." Lazarus's voice was rough with desire.

"Promises, promises," Ivy said silkily and hopped off the stool. As she passed, she kissed him, and his cock throbbed in response. "I'll see you upstairs."

"Meet me, hell, I'm coming with you."

Lazarus swept her into his arms, and her laughter made him grin as he made a beeline for the stairs. The rest of breakfast was forgotten when he slid her down his hard body, and his shirt rode up her body, he could feel her soft skin. It was a little while later before they left for a day in San Diego. One step closer, Lazarus thought while they sat in the plush leather seats of the jet. He wasn't going to be cocky and say he won the game and Ivy because he knew there were underlying players, and they still had moves on the board.

Chapter Seven

Ivy wasn't a hummer; in fact, she liked to paint with only the music pulsing around her, and it was usually death metal. Today, she painted what she considered a serene abstract of nature that consisted of a winter ice storm. Cool colors kept her eyes fixed on the canvas as she blurred the trees and the mountaintops in the background. She wanted to keep the shapes and the definition of each object on the canvas but give it a sense of whimsy.

She ended up spending the rest of the weekend with Lazarus, and he dropped her off at her apartment early Monday morning before he went into his office for the day. He promised someone would bring her car from his house later in the afternoon, which was fine because she didn't plan to go anywhere. Their lovemaking had left her sated, and she thought she would go home to sleep but instead inspiration struck her. Now she painted with a zealousness that she loved. She heard a pounding knock before the loft door slid open and Trent walked in.

"I've been calling you all weekend," he said instantly.

"Sorry, phone's been dead," she answered.

He gave her his charming smile and held up his hands. "I forgive you. I figured you got into the zone to work. I bring coffee and bagels for us to share, then maybe we can go to some galleries and spend the day together."

"I'm not hungry. I'm just happy to be working on this right now." Ivy smiled and focused on her art.

"Awww, come on, you had to be working all weekend. Take a break," Trent said. "We have barely seen each other in the last week."

"Sorry Trent, give me a few days," Ivy said apologetically. "I'm in my own head right now and liking it."

He stepped closer to look at the piece. "This is new for you, very soft and feminine."

She chuckled. "I am a woman."

"But for you, even the music is soft…" She turned to get more paint on her brush just in time to see him frown. "Why do I smell Vale all over you?"

"I thought you didn't use your shifter senses?" Ivy asked pointedly.

"You can hardly miss it, and it's not like I'm sniffing you like a dog does a hydrant," Trent said stiffly. "Why do you smell like him?"

"You're being nosy but if this is need to know information for you, we spent the weekend together," she said simply and went back to work.

"Are you kidding me!" Trent shouted. "You called me pissed at a contract, and you end up sleeping with the guy?"

"Why the hell are you raising your voice at me?" Ivy retorted. "We weren't thinking about the contract this weekend, it will be sorted out. Lazarus and I made this great connection over the past few days, and I want to see where it goes."

"Ah you idiot, you *ho-ra!*" Trent threw the coffee at her painting and grabbed her shoulders and shook her. "I didn't think you were so stupid! Ivy, you're a commodity to him, nothing more. I hope it was a good fuck because he will use you and toss you aside."

Ivy looked at her ruined painting. The coffee dripped between the white paint, making it run and blend. It pooled in a mess on the floor, and her anger rose. *How dare he?* He spoke to her like she was some stupid girl, called her a whore in Norwegian that she didn't know he spoke, and presumed she was being used…

Does he think I'm some bubblehead, cheap… oh, am I whore now? He had his hand on me and he shook me… This was more than anger, it rippled beneath her skin and threatened to burst free. Ripping his throat out with her teeth was almost too pleasurable a thought. She wanted to see his blood on her lips.

"Take your hands off me." Her voice was low and emphasized each word.

Trent looked down and frowned. "What's going on with your eyes?"

"Remove your hands before I do something we will both regret," Ivy said again, and she could hear the harsh undertones in her own voice. "You presume because we are friends that you can treat me however, speak to me however, and destroy my work? You call me a whore like you've ever touched my body to be jealous or know what I can do. TAKE YOUR HANDS OFF ME!"

She snarled the words, and he scrambled back. Trent held up his hands, and she moved toward him slowly, stalking him, because at that point he was her prey.

"Ivy, calm down, I—I'm sorry I messed up the painting, I'll clean it all up, I'm sorry for what I said," he babbled. "We're friends, you're my best friend."

"Yet you talk to me like I'm some kind of baseborn bitch," she snapped. "Get out, before I swear to God I kill you."

Trent laughed nervously. "Ivy, you'd never hurt me. Come on, calm down, and I'll take you to lunch. Let me apologize the right way. You know I care for you and love you."

"That's the only thing that's keeping you alive... you care," she said slowly and took a breath trying to control herself, scared of what she was feeling. "Leave now. I won't ask again."

She heard the door of her loft close, and she sank into the chair on shaking feet. *What's going on with me?* She wondered if Lazarus and his wolf nature was rubbing off on her. She'd read that even humans could feel the effects of a wolf alpha's power indirectly. Maybe that was it, some hormone in him was making her wild. Even so, she felt like she was crawling out of her skin and couldn't calm down. She found her phone on the charger, called Lazarus's number, and was relieved when he answered on the first ring.

"Hi, do you miss me already?" His voice was charming and smooth on the phone.

"Are—are you busy, can you come back?" she asked hearing the desperation in her own voice.

His tone became alarmed. "Ivy, what's going on?"

"Trent, he was upset... and..." She took a deep breath, trying to force herself to be calm. "Just come please."

"What did he do?" Lazarus's voice roared across the phone, and she whimpered because it made her feel even wilder. "I'm on my way."

He hung up, and she move from her seat to pace. Ivy honestly felt like she was losing it. Lazarus had to know something to counteract what she was feeling. God, she hoped they could put in some kind of parameters in place before moving forward. Ivy didn't think she could handle having these feelings if she was upset. She felt like she was on a PMS roller coaster ride after taking a steroid shot. She didn't know how long she paced but when he dragged the door open and slammed it behind him before he strode in, she breathed a sigh of relief.

"Where is the baseborn mutt—I will kill him, rip his mangy head from his body!" Lazarus's eyes flashed yellow, and his body was hunched over and tensed like he was ready to pounce.

"It's nothing, it's me, he's gone." Ivy took a deep breath. "It's not helping that you're so amped up. He came over here and smelled you on me. He threw coffee on my painting... Then grabbed me..."

"I will rip his arms from his body," Lazarus growled.

"No!" Ivy cried out. "It's me! I was so mad I wanted to kill him. I never felt anything so primal and violent before. I was so mad it felt like it was crawling under my skin. Lazarus, what is going on? I heard it in my voice... If this is some remnant of your ability then we need to figure out how to stop it."

"Ivy, that's not how it works." Lazarus came toward her slowly and stroked her shoulders gently. "I can only affect my people, not you, even as my mate. It's something else, something in you."

"There's nothing in me. I'm human," she said.

"Your father chose to live in our world, maybe there's a reason," Lazarus hinted.

"My dad would have told me if there was anything." Ivy walked into his arms and pressed her face against the fabric of his suit. "It's crazy how I feel..."

Lazarus rocked her gently. "It's okay, I'm here."

The urges within her changed, and she lifted her nose to his neck and inhaled his scent. Her arousal kicked in, and she felt her essence pool between her legs and soak her panties. Lazarus growled, and she knew he'd scented her arousal.

Ivy stood on her tiptoes and kissed him ravenously. She whimpered in delight when he took over the kiss, and they became frantic with need. She pushed at his coat until he shrugged out of it and it dropped to the floor. Ivy was pulling his tie off, and she worked at the buttons of his shirt, growling in frustration when her fingers didn't work fast enough.

"Rip it, I don't care," Lazarus muttered against her lips.

Buttons flew everywhere with the force she used when she pulled his shirt apart. Ivy gasped as she felt his hand under her loose sundress kneading the skin of her ass before he reached around and slid his hand into her panties. She bucked against his hand with a loud cry when his finger probed and found her core. He sank his digits deep within her, and she could feel her thick juice cream against his fingers and run down her legs.

"Oh fuck yes," he growled against her ear. "You're so hot and wet, I want more of you."

He grabbed the silky fabric of her panties, and it frayed and tore under his grasp. They were close to the window seat, and Ivy knew if anyone could see in, they would get an eyeful. She got his belt undone and his pants dropped to the floor. She expected boxers but found nothing, making it easy for her to take the width of his cock in her grasp and stroke his rock hard length.

"You went commando," she said with a breathless laugh.

"Always ready for you, my sweet girl."

He lifted her into his arms, and her dress bunched up around her waist and between them as he sat down in the window seat. She felt his cock at the entrance to her pussy and sank down onto the rod slowly. He was so thick. She bit her lip and moaned gently as he sank deeper into her, loving the way he stretched the walls of her sex. The velvety steel feel of him almost drove her to madness, and she undulated her hips slowly, loving how his breath hissed out from between his clenched teeth.

"You are so tight, ah shit baby, don't move like that, not yet," he groaned.

She bit his lip in an aggressive move. "I love how you feel inside me, let's fuck hard and fast."

"God, I love when you say dirty things," he muttered. "Ride me, let me feel you come all over my cock."

She bit his neck as his hands gripped her hips tight, and he lifted his hips thrusting into her hard. The feel of him inside her only fueled her primal need as she moved to meet his rhythm. He fucked her with a wildness that she had come to crave in only a short time. Lazarus pulled the front of her dress savagely, ripping it so that he could get to her breasts. She cried out his name as he enclosed one pert tip into his hot mouth as he moved.

Ivy rode him harder, faster, as the sensation pulsed through her core, driving her toward her release. She screamed his name as she came hard, her pussy clenching around his cock. His loud, grunting groan heralded his own release, and the feel of his hot seed filling the cavern of her sex gave her immense satisfaction. It was only then that she felt sated, and the wildness that was within seemed to ebb like the tide going back out to sea. She leaned her head against his shoulder as he kicked his pants off and lifted her gently in his arms.

"Do you have to go back to work?" she asked.

"I will in a little while." He kissed her as he lay her in bed. "I want to hold you just a little longer."

"Like when wolves sleep together warm in a den." She sighed.

"Just like that," he chuckled.

"It seems only you can ease the wildness in me. I don't understand why it's happening to me, I'm human," she said sleepily.

"We'll figure it out," he said. "Sleep, love."

"Okay."

She sighed in contentment, loving his scent as it surrounded her and made her feel complete. Ivy drifted off to sleep with the thought that even though she was human, being mated to him was a definite plus.

Chapter Eight

A week passed, and she hadn't spoken to Trent. They'd never gone so long without talking, and she missed him—they were best friends. But she wasn't ready to forgive the things he said or what he had done. He called her a whore, in Norwegian no less. That wasn't his birthright unless he had read up on the language. *People always learn the bad words of a new language first, that's all.*

She played it over every which way in her head but couldn't find a solution on why he would act that way. They'd never been anything more than friends, and to be honest, not seeing him with anyone usually made her think he was gay. She never broached the subject because if he wanted her to know he'd tell her, and it wasn't her business. It wouldn't make a difference because she loved him, but jealousy over her relationship with Lazarus? It still floored her.

Now she was in the car with Lazarus, and they sped away from the city toward Muir

Woods. He told her that the location of the main house the pack used for meeting was there, and that was their destination. Her stomach clenched nervously. Why had she accepted to go? He wanted her to meet the pack as his mate but she didn't know if she was ready for that or the fact that he'd committed himself to her so completely. There were so many variables, obstacles that could stand between them, and the main one was the primal feelings that Ivy was convinced were caused by Lazarus. Yet she was in his car, and he drove seamlessly using one hand to steer and the other to hold her hand.

"You don't have to worry." Lazarus lifted her hand and kissed it. "It's very informal."

"Do you sit in the 'grand poobah' chair, and they come to your feet with their issues?" Ivy asked.

Lazarus laughed. "You have a very skewed notion about how pack life works."

"Pardon me, but I've never been to one of these things. Humans aren't usually allowed, am I correct?" Ivy pointed out. "Plus, it's not like Dad and Eric have been invited to Kristoff's round table meetings."

"I understand what you mean," Lazarus said. "Like I said, informal. We sit around a big bonfire and eat. Then grab a beer or two with each other, and as people need to talk to me, they come over to the picnic table all casual like."

"Understood. Do I sit beside you and stroke your neck?" Ivy teased.

"That would be appreciated." Lazarus grinned.

She punched his arm. "Next you'll want me to call you my liege."

"Nothing so formal. My king, the conqueror of my body, would suffice," he answered.

"Yeah, you may be waiting a long time for that one," she replied.

She didn't see the driveway when he turned because it was hidden between tall trees. There was no lighting along the gravel path, and Ivy understood that they probably didn't want anyone to notice the lights from the road and turning on to their property. Keeping the secret of their second nature was tantamount among the packs because an innocent human wandering into their territory would not end well.

The lights from the Land Rover highlighted the outside of the house. *House*, she thought derisively. It was more like a rustic ski lodge with high glass windows set in the log cabin design. Even in the dark, she could see the landscaping was immaculately kept in the front, set with rock walls around the flower beds to blend in with the natural look. There were at least two dozen cars parked all over the large front yard.

"You said informal pack grounds, not palatial mountain mansion," Ivy said. Lazarus stopped the car and walked around to the passenger side door to open it.

"Some pack members live here on and off, and they are all welcome," Lazarus explained. "I don't usually know who's living here when I show up. Last time I showed up Rachel was giving birth to our newest pack member. She wasn't comfortable anywhere else, and the three pups she and Hank already have almost tripped me up."

"Families are here as well," she said as he took her hand and they walked around to the back of the house. She could already hear laughter and happy chatter when they approached, and it made her all the more nervous.

Lazarus gave her a look. "The pack is built on family, unity — without it, we are nothing."

It seemed when they arrived everyone knew because all eyes turned to them. She recognized Silvia, Luca, and two other faces who had been with Lazarus before. But the multitude of people staring was disconcerting. She estimated them to be at least fifty.

"Hey everyone, I hope the food is good," Lazarus said with a grin.

The relaxed comment was met with a round of hellos, and people went back to what they were doing. She could still sense the curiosity around them about who she was. Silvia walked up to them as Lazarus directed Ivy with his hand on her back to a table devoid of anyone else sitting there. Silvia wore a pair of black jeans and a blue sweat top. *Is there anything she wears that doesn't like a supermodel on a runway,* Ivy thought. She moved like a sleek cat and sat with grace across from Lazarus and looked at her.

"Well, look at you all clothed," Silvia drawled the teasing words.

"Hopefully that was the last time you see me naked," Ivy replied.

Silvia grinned. "Saucy, I like that. You'll need it with some of these bitches."

"Excuse me?" Ivy said.

"You know, bitches, females in heat and looking at our Alpha as their…"

"Silvia…" Lazarus warned.

"Just saying, Raven is here," Silvia commented smoothly. "I'll go grab you a plate, Ivy. Luca will bring you something, boss."

"Thank you," Ivy said as Silvia walked away, and she turned her attention to Lazarus. "Who is this Raven?"

"An unattached female who wants us to be

mated," Lazarus answered, and her eyes widened in surprise. "Did you expect me to lie?"

"No, just not so forthcoming," she answered.

He lifted her hand on the table and kissed her palm before closing it around his hand. The action was done in view of everyone, and she had no doubt that it was a calculated move to show they were connected. Silvia came back with a plate laden with food, so much that Ivy knew she wouldn't be able to eat it all. But she looked around and noticed that even the women ate heartily.

"We have big appetites," Silvia commented noticing her look. "Our bodies run hotter, and our metabolism burns through energy at a high rate."

"But I'm human, I can't eat all this," Ivy pointed out.

"Eat what you can," Silvia said and sat down to her own plate.

As they ate, she half listened to their conversation and devoured her food. She was hungrier than she thought. People came up with chairs or sometimes stood to discuss issues with Lazarus or ask for his counsel. He was always fair, gave people the benefit of the doubt until they were proven wrong. Then he offered solutions that didn't give favor to anyone, it just was fair.

One man walked up, looking haggard and rumpled in clothes that hadn't seen a washing for a few days. His beard had grown out, and his eyes were bloodshot and weary. He stood in front of Lazarus silently, waiting for permission to speak. Ivy sense a change in the small group at the table. Even Silvia went quiet and focused on her food.

"Josh," Lazarus said his name cordially. "How are you tonight?"

"How do I look, Lazarus?" Josh snapped. "I come to ask leave of the Vale pack and help relocating."

"Why, Josh? You can still have a good life here, plenty of other viable…" Lazarus began.

"No!" Josh yelled, and the entire pack quieted, looking in their direction. "I cannot live in a pack where she is. She left our mating bond to move on with William. Am I supposed to sit and watch them eat and kiss without feeling something?"

"Josh, we never meant to hurt you. We were just not the right fit," a woman stepped up and said.

Josh glared at her with hurt in his eyes. "Wolves mate for life but not you, huh, Betty? William may be in my position sooner than he thinks when you want to move one more step up the pack chain. I was just a lowly worker, and now you are with an enforcer, so fuck the bond."

"It's not like that," William said.

"Don't you talk to me," Josh roared and turned back to Lazarus. "I want to leave, and with or without your blessing I plan to do so. I just want what is fairly mine and your word that when I join a new pack and the Alpha contacts you, you'll give the blessing for me to be there."

Lazarus sighed. "I understand. I can only imagine what you are going through. Nor can I tell Betty what she and William have formed is not sanctioned. The bond was broken between you — I felt it break, and it will never return. I give you permission to leave the Vale pack, and you will leave with the financial means to restart where you choose. You have my word that I will speak highly to any new potential pack leader that you are a solid good man and wolf. May you be well, Josh. The pack can offer you their goodbyes."

"I want none," Josh said and turned on his heels to leave.

Betty turned her face into William's shoulder and cried softly. Ivy could see anger on some faces and disappointment at Josh leaving. This new union had caused a rift between those who supported the new couple and those who believed Josh was wronged.

Lazarus stood up, and his voice carried across the large back yard. "This will not be the thing that divides us. One bond is broken, another has been formed. Josh made his choice, and we will abide by it. I want no dissention in the Vale pack or anger against Betty and William because of it."

"I have an issue with one who is not part of our pack among us," a woman stood and spoke.

Ivy looked at her curiously. The breeze ruffled her dark hair, and the hostile, hateful look she threw in Ivy's direction only cemented the fact that this was Raven.

"You bring a human amongst us and openly show affection to her," Raven said loudly. "When, as you said yourself, there are perfectly viable females in the pack."

"Your concern is noted, Raven. Ivy's family has always lived among shifters, and they have all kept the secrets," Lazarus explained mildly. "She is fine to me here, and as my mate she is welcomed."

"What kind of Alpha chooses to dilute our blood with a human?" Raven spat out.

"Are you challenging me, Raven?" Lazarus asked, and as he stood Ivy saw his eyes flash yellow. "Do you want to lead the pack?"

"No Lazarus, she is not." An older woman

tried to grab Raven to sit down, and the young woman shook off her hand angrily.

"No one is brave enough to speak but I will," Raven said hotly. "I have offered myself up as your mate but you refused. I can give you family, healthy boys and girls to make the pack stronger. I do not want to fight my alpha but if the human wants you, she should fight me with honor to do so, like the old ways."

Some people murmured an agreement, and Lazarus let out a roar of anger that seemed to reverberate through all of them, including her. She felt the magic of the pack, the bonds that connected them to their Alpha as he pulled them to his will and showed them why his word, his actions, protected them all. He was the strongest, the true Alpha, and he would not be disobeyed. How could she feel his pull in the blood coursing along her veins?

Ivy gasped and arched as it ran along her back and seemed to infuse her spine. She looked across the table and all around to see Silvia, Lucas, all of their eyes were yellow as the wolf within them was at the cusp of being released. Lazarus could force their shift with his power, but that was his pack. Why did she feel his will and see him in her mind? A black wolf, a dark blur as he ran through the trees, and when he stopped and faced her, the yellow eyes of his black wolf seemed to penetrate her.

"You were never going to be my mate, Raven, regardless of Ivy. Your childish ways of thinking about yourself over pack, being led by a viper's tongue and jealous intentions sealed that in stone," Lazarus said angrily. When he spoke again, his voice was harsh, and no one met his gaze. "Then you dare to presume to challenge my mate after my decision? Remember who you are, Raven, and to all of you I say this: Any challenge I will answer on behalf of Ivy, and I will not show mercy to anyone… not even you, Raven."

He almost buckled the entire pack with the force of his will. Silvia looked at Ivy, and when she spoke her voice had a hard tinge, as if she was fighting a losing battle against her body shifting.

"Calm him," Silvia said though gritted teeth.

Ivy reached up a shaky hand and put it on his forearm. Lazarus looked down at her, and she pleaded with him, using her eyes. She was finding it hard to speak, let alone understand what was coursing through her. He stared down at her, and she watched as his eyes changed from the wolf to human once more. He took a deep breath and unclenched his fists before sitting back down and turning his attention to his food. Silvia sat up with a sigh and pulled down the front of her shirt, neatly smoothing it out.

"Thanks," she said and took a forkful of potato salad.

Ivy looked at her incredulously. All of them were acting like they hadn't buckled under the weight of the Alpha's will. What bothered her most of all was that it had affected her, and the fact that she was able to calm him. Without saying a word, she stood and walked away from the table and headed toward the car.

"Ivy," he called, but she didn't stop her forward momentum to the car. He caught up to her and swung her around to face him.

"I want to go home," she said stiffly.

"Ivy, I'm sorry about what she said," Lazarus replied.

"It's not about her, it's the fact that you affect me like I'm one of your pack, and I'm a freaking human being!" she yelled.

"Calm down." He pulled her into his arms and hugged her. "I think maybe you have some latent wolf in you, and it's opening up because you're with me."

"My family is human, no wolf within us," she said adamantly.

"Maybe you should talk to your father about that," Lazarus said gently.

"You say that like you know something," Ivy said warily.

"No more than you, and even if I did, it isn't mine to tell," Lazarus answered. "Talk to your father, and maybe he can shed some light as to what is going on. But not now I'll show you upstairs to my rooms, and you can relax. You'll be far enough away so when we shift it shouldn't bother you."

"It shouldn't affect me," she muttered. "You don't seem to be getting this fact."

He kissed her temple as he walked her to the house. "I know, sweetheart, I understand all too well. You're scared, and you don't know why."

"Exactly." She sighed, suddenly feeling very tired.

"See, I get it." Upstairs, he helped her undress and got her under the thick blankets in his bed.

"You always seem to be putting me to bed," she said sleepily.

"Only once or twice," He chuckled softly and pressed a kiss on her lips. "Now sleep, and I promise not to wake you when I come in."

"You said that last time and next thing you know... naked," she replied. "Lazarus..."

She never finished her words as the darkness of sleep took over.

Lazarus rejoined the pack. Silvia. along with Luca and two others of his enforcers, were now sitting at the table. He sat down and quietly ate, pondering why Raven thought that it would be so easy to challenge Ivy in front of the pack. Was he getting soft or was she that stupid?

"She's not all there and jealousy makes anyone brave," Silvia said, as if reading his mind.

"She needs someone to give her attention to," Luca said.

"Are you putting yourself up for nomination?" Andy one of the other enforcers, asked.

Luca grunted before speaking. "Hell no, she wants a lap dog that will trot along and do her bidding."

"That's definitely not Lazarus or any of us," Mikal said. "Did she really think being the Alpha's mate would give her influence over the pack?"

"She'd like to think that," Lazarus said. "What did you find out?"

"About the break in or the fact that we saw her eyes when you used the pack bonds to show your will?" Silvia said.

"She is what you expected her to be," Luca said.

"I'm not worried about that now. Even if she was human, I'm already mated to her," Lazarus said.

"But a big bonus that she is," Silvia said. "In any case, we found who broke in, and your little mutt is a part of it. He saw an older man, and he had the papers stolen by the baseborn."

"Who's the old man?" Lazarus asked.

"I think maybe it's the mutt's father, but why would he want papers about Ivy's heritage?" Luca said.

"Because he knows what she is and the importance of that fact. The baseborns are making a play for the board," Lazarus said. "They're tired of being the low man on the totem pole, and they think Ivy is the way to get it."

"So the old man is using the mutt as a mate possibility?" Silvia laughed till tears were in her eyes.

"It's no laughing matter," Lazarus said quietly. "When he found out that she was with me, he destroyed her painting and came at her in her loft. This man is expecting that their friendship will lead to something more, and then they will have the power."

"We should kill them all now," Mikal snarled.

"No, this has to be played out the right way. The choice has to be hers, and she doesn't know what she is yet. How can she choose until she knows?" Lazarus said.

"Then tell her," Silvia insisted.

"This story has to be heard from her father." Lazarus met their gazes. "We say nothing until our part of the story comes into play."

"Your father knew and look where that got him," Luca said. "The truth can always be hidden in a mountain of lies."

"It can be, but she's the type of person who will dig for the truth so the lies will be inconsequential," Lazarus said. "For now, we wait."

"We run," Mikal said, getting up and stretching. "I feel the need to run off this food. The moon is high in the sky, and she calls to us."

"She calls to us," Lazarus agreed, stood, and announced loudly. "Tonight, we run!"

A pleased murmur ran through the pack, and they eagerly removed their clothes. Even Raven who managed to know her place seemed ready to shed her human skin and become one with their surroundings. Lazarus led the pack as they moved through the woods around them. Everything was clean and crisp; the night sky was clear, and the night was filled with more life than any human could imagine. He was the night, the wolf that embraced the darkness around him. Even in his second nature, he thought about Ivy and all the potential variables that could take her from him. The thought made him angry, and he ran all the faster, leaving even his fastest enforcer in the dust. He would do anything to keep her, and every obstacle in his path would feel his teeth at their neck before he let them take Ivy from him.

Chapter Nine

She couldn't deny it any longer. Ivy knew she had to speak to her father. She hadn't spoken to them since the last blow out, and as she drove toward their new apartment she grimaced. It seemed like she and everyone she loved was on the outs lately. She still felt resentment that instead of driving to their trailer she was heading to a duplex on Union Street to see her dad. Could she blame him?

He wanted something better in life, and that was perfectly fine, but Ivy still felt like a pawn used to help them get ahead. Her father never tried to raise his status while she was growing up and to her this was an easy way out. She pushed away the rising the irritation inside her. There were more pressing matters at hand. Ivy parked and walked the small distance to their new home, noting the nice park across the street and the laughter of kids in the air. It was a good area, much better than the crime ridden trailer park.

She rang the doorbell, noting that this was the first time she didn't have a key to let herself in.

Her father opened the door with a wide smile. "Babygirl, it is good to see your pretty face."

"Hi dad." Ivy's heart warmed at her father's face. He had tried his best, and she couldn't ask him to be something he was not. "How are you? Has Eric been helping with dinners?"

He nodded as he took her hand and ushered her inside. "Oh *wi*, he has and has even tried to make stir fry."

Ivy smiled. "How was it?"

"He is not a chef, let's put it that way. He is asleep in his bedroom," her father answered as he pulled her into his arms. "I have missed you, Ivy. Let's not fight anymore."

She returned his embrace and pressed her nose into his scratchy shirt. "No more arguing, but Dad, I have questions about my life. Strange things have been happening."

He pulled away and frowned at her. "Strange things?"

Ivy crossed the room and sat on the new black leather sofa. "Dad, does our family have any wolf shifters in it, maybe like a great aunt or uncle?"

"Why?" Ivy noted as her father said the word, he looked away quickly and folded his calloused hand in his lap.

"When I am with Lazarus, I can feel his power, the alpha in him." She leaned forward intently. "At a pack meeting, he had to quell a disturbance, and he did something. I almost felt like I was crawling out of my skin."

Her father grinned. "It is going well if you were allowed to go to his pack home."

Ivy sighed. "Focus on my questions, please. I need to know what's inside me, if anything, or have we been living with shifters for so long that it's starting to rub off?"

"It's not that." Her father sighed. "I never thought we'd have this conversation. Your mother hoped that it would never come, and if it did, she could speak to you before she died."

Ivy felt like cold water had been thrown in her face, and she gasped in reaction to her father's words. He never really spoke about their mother, and she could barely remember her. Eric was a baby when she died so he had no memory of her.

"What am I, Dad?" Ivy said quietly, as if the words would shatter all she knew.

"You are the last white wolf. You are royalty. You are not only my princess, you are an actual princess," her father said. "And I am not your father."

Ivy stared at him in shock. "No, you rocked me to sleep, you took me to my first day of school. Wolves first shift at puberty, and I'm thirty years old... How can I be..."

The questions blurred together in her mind, and she stopped talking. She never broke eye contact with her father. Willing her to tell her this was a joke, and she could be mad at first then they could laugh together about it. But his eyes told her this was reality, and there was much she didn't know.

"Once upon a time there was a young princess who fell in love with another," her father said and smiled sadly. "This was your mother, and the man she loved was not me, he was my best friend. He came to St. Lucia long ago, and we fished together, then I met his wife—your mother. I never knew that black women lived in Norway but there she was, a queen among us. She was a descendant from one of the old tribes of Africa who found their place in Norway instead of facing slavery. Her eyes were the color of yours, and it made her an exotic treasure, because of her beauty and the fact it was the mark of the white wolf, a rarity in the entire world. In Norway, they flourished but were always at a disadvantage."

Her father's hand shook as he spoke. "Your mother was amazing, kind, and full of life. But she was afraid. Her father had arranged a marriage with another pack, and this would cement a treaty between them. The packs would combine and become powerful, but your mother loved Agnor, another from her tribe, and they planned to run away to America. St. Lucia was a stop, and then I became part of the family. I traveled with them, and your mother and father were willing to give up everything to be with each other."

"What happened?" Ivy asked through numb lips.

"Her father found out and with the leader of the other pack found them and killed Agnor a few weeks after we got to America," he answered sadly. "As he died in our arms, he begged me to get your mother to safety. They both knew her new husband and the pack would treat her cruelly for going against them. I dragged her away from his body covered in blood, and we continued the journey without him. She didn't know that she was carrying their child, created with love. Zoya had you within her belly."

Silent tears slipped down her cheeks, and her father, or the man she always thought of as her Da, came to sit on the sofa next to her and pulled her against him as he leaned back. Ivy listened as he spoke—the story needed to be told.

"In America, we thought it best to hide who

she was, but we also knew we needed the protection of a pack so she didn't become crazed with the loss of a pack bond, so we settled here," her father continued. "Being a royal wolf meant she could mask certain things, especially from lesser wolves, so no one ever knew."

"How did she die?" Ivy's voice was choked with tears.

"Someone found out who she was and tried to rip her away from me, a lowly human," he explained. "Before that we both knew that if someone was to ever find out who she was, or the fact that you may have the blood within you, both you and she would be taken and forced to marry so they could claim all that is rightfully yours. So we had another child, Eric, so no one could tell which child may be the next royal, since they thought you were my daughter. Having a child with a human means it is a fifty percent chance you could have the wolf within or not. Your mother bound your second nature so you wouldn't shift when you came of age, and only a true alpha could bring it from within."

"Do you know who killed her?" Ivy asked. It all seemed like a horrible dream, a fairy tale filled with darkness, sorrow and death.

"I never knew. I assumed it was one of the districts alphas but could never be sure," her father explained. "I came home to find her in bed with her neck snapped, and you being so young, holding Eric in your tiny arms, crying at the foot of the bed. I know you saw who it was but because you were so young you could never remember. You had such horrible nightmares for a long time. I spun the story that your mother died peacefully to replace what you had seen, and slowly your child's mind began to believe my story of a nightmare, nothing more, until the dreams stopped."

"They never really stopped." Ivy looked up at him. "I just got better at hiding them. The dark monster over Eric and me never really went away. I just hated seeing your worry, so I kept it to myself."

"I should've known." Her father cupped her cheek and smiled. "Now you know. You are royalty, and what is within you is trying to be free to be with its mate, Lazarus."

"And I'm what, the son born to protect her secret?" Eric's voice came from behind them, filled with anger. When she looked up to see him standing on the stairs that led to the bedrooms his eyes were a storm of rage and hurt. "So that's the secret, dad? She's the princess, and I'm her lowly deadbeat brother?"

"Eric no!" Ivy cried out and surged to her feet

as he came into the room. "You are loved. You are my brother, and you're…"

"I'm nothing, an afterthought to make sure no one knew what you truly are." He sneered at his father. "You were sloppy seconds, Pop. She loved someone else and only let you fuck her to make a kid to protect the golden child."

"Never speak of your mother that way!" Her father surged to his feet. "She loved us all. After her grief came the love and the family she adored. Your birth was one of the happiest moments of her life."

"Keep thinking that, Dad, so it gets you through the night," Eric said coldly. "Why am I here, anyway? I've got money in the bank, and obviously this family isn't what I thought it was. I'll get my last check and my part of the cash from Ivy being sold out to Vale and be on my way." He gave a hollow laugh. "I always wondered why you favored her, why I felt like I lived in her shadow. Now I know why. I need some air, then I'll come grab my shit and leave."

"Eric please, stop." Ivy was openly crying now and grabbed his arm. "This isn't our fault. We knew nothing about it, and it was all planned without us knowing."

He looked down at her hand and then at her with anger in his eyes. "Yet you come out of this smelling like a rose while I'm still the guy working on the docks stinking of fish."

He shrugged her hand off and stalked out the door. Ivy was about to go after him when her father stopped her.

"Don't—let him blow off his steam," he said gently and cupped her cheek. "You've also learned your true heritage today, and there are some things of your mother's that are now yours. I may not have been your real father, but I have done right by you the best I could. Now it's time to claim your birthright."

Ivy hugged him tight. "No matter who made me, in my heart and in every way that counts you have been my Dad."

Ivy left an hour later with a small chest that held her mother's birth certificate, her royal titles, some small pieces of jewelry, and other mementos. Buried in the depths was a picture of her real father as well. The light turned red, and she slowed to a stop at the intersection and looked at the image. He was tall, and her mother looked up at him with a look of adoration. He'd died for them, and the man she knew as father took up the charge to keep them safe.

Two heroes and no clues about who killed her mother, who could've known her secret and caused her death because of it. It was all too much, and instead of going home she turned her little Miata toward Lazarus's home. He wasn't there, and she doubted he would be for a while yet, but he had given her free reign of his home. She walked into the airy foyer and made sure to arm the security system behind her.

I need a glass of wine, she thought. After all she'd learned, she wondered if Lazarus kept vodka in the house. *Probably not, last time it was that god awful whiskey.* She went into the kitchen and grabbed a bottle of wine and then put it back and opted for champagne. *No vodka or gin, I'll make it work.* She shrugged. Lazarus probably kept it light because alcohol and shifters sometimes didn't mix well. *We don't need a drunk wolf on the Golden Gate bridge howling at the moon.* She laughed to herself at her joke and quickly became somber.

She was one of those shifters, and the feeling inside her was second nature waking from her lifetime of slumber. *Will I be able to control it? Will it hurt when I shift to a wolf?* Ivy used the electronic opener to remove the cork. With the box her father gave her under her arm, Ivy took the whole bottle of the bubby with her to the bedroom and sat crossed legged in the middle of Lazarus's bed to go through the small box that held her birthright. That's how Lazarus found her a few hours later, the bottle of champagne almost gone, and Ivy more than pleasantly buzzed. At some point she put aside the pictures and letters, the titles, deeds, and hell, even a bankbook. Now she watched cartoons on the massive TV on the wall and peered at him owlishly when he walked through the door.

"I've been calling you, and I went by your loft," he commented as he loosened his tie. "What'cha doing?"

"I've been here having a party, a celebration of sorts," Ivy replied and moved clumsily to kneel in the middle of the bed after she grabbed the bottle from the bedside table and took a swing from the champagne. "Guess what."

"Since you are drinking alone and without a glass, I don't think it's good." Lazarus sat on the edge of the bed and pushed the box. "What's all this?"

Ivy spread her arms wide and gave him a wide grin. "My celebration, my heritage so to speak. Hey, you never guessed."

"I did, and I give up so now you have to tell me," Lazarus said gently.

She didn't remember him answering but gave him the benefit of the doubt.

"Well, it seems you were right. I do have

shifter blood, and it's this big to do with my family," Ivy said conspiratorially. "There's love, death, murder..."

"Who got murdered?" Lazarus asked with a dark look on his face.

"My mother was murdered because she was African wolf royalty who found refuge in Norway," Ivy answered. "Apparently, I am princess wolf, and get this—Eric was born to make sure no one could tell which one of us would have the blood line."

"Fascinating. What else did you find out?" he asked.

"Other than that, I can claim deeds, lands, and apparently money in Norwegian..."

"Norway," he corrected.

"Potato, Po-tah-to." Ivy waved her arm airily. "In any case, from what I read, I have to be able to shift into a wolf to claim it. And all that I have been feeling when I'm around you is my wolf waking up."

Lazarus grinned. "Glad I could help. I could probably push it along if you want."

"I don't want to hurt," Ivy said, suddenly afraid. "I don't even know if I want this at all. I have lived all my life without these... these... feelings, and this has turned my world upside down! Eric is gone, and now I'm some royalty who owns stuff and people killed my mother. Who could wrap their heads around that?"

"Don't think about it now." Lazarus plucked the bottle from her hand and put it on the ground. "How about we get some food into you and some rest. You can think more clearly on it tomorrow. You could paint, it gives you clarity when you let yourself go in your work."

Ivy beamed at him. "You really get me."

He smiled gently. "I try."

Ivy tackled him on the bed, and the momentum took them to the floor. He landed on his back with an "oof" as it knocked the breath from his lungs. Lazarus held her to him to protect her from hitting the carpet with him. She scrambled up so she was straddling his body and began to finish the job of removing his tie and unbuttoning his shirt.

"What are you doing?" he asked, amused.

"Helping you undress so we can put something other than food inside me," she replied wickedly and wiggled on his lap.

"I think you may be too drunk to take on this wolf," he teased but she could hear the arousal in his voice.

"I would've been much worse if you had vodka." She nipped his chin. "I want you, Lazarus, take what's yours."

He cupped his hand in her hair and looked at her. "So you admit, you are my mate, you submit?"

"I submit to you wolf," Ivy whispered. "Don't hurt me, and don't force me to do something I'm not ready for."

He kissed her hand and growled. "Never."

Ivy stripped off her knit top and took off her bra. "Then take me because I am yours."

He said her name huskily before he took her lips in a kiss that made her toes curl. Lazarus covered her with his body, and she wrapped her legs around his waist. He pinned her arms over her head as he speared his tongue into her mouth. All she could feel was his lips against hers and the way he made her feel, wild and untamed yet loved and cherished at them same time. He tasted so delectable, a man shouldn't taste like he did, and she could kiss him for hours without a problem. His lips ravished hers, and Ivy feasted on him in return She wanted more, God, she wanted more from him, everything, his all.

"You are my all," he muttered against her lips. His fingers worked on the waist of her skirt.

She grabbed his head and pulled him away. "How did you know what I thought?"

He shrugged. "Sometimes it happens, especially if we are mated."

She was finally free of the confines of her clothes and Lazarus turned and lifted her over him so her breasts were ripe and full above his mouth. He took her nipple into his mouth like he was tasting grapes from the bunch. Ivy gasped in pleasure and arched her back, pushing her smooth globes deeper into his mouth.

"Oh yes, I love how your mouth feels on my skin," she moaned, and Lazarus groaned in response.

"I have to taste you, I can smell your nectar, it makes me insatiable," he said gutturally.

Ivy pulled away and leaned back so her hands were on the carpet between his legs. She spread the velvet folds of her sex with her fingers, revealing it to his gaze.

"Then come taste me, every... last... drop," she whispered.

Lazarus needed no other invitation. He moved so quickly she gasped when he pulled her hips to his mouth roughly. He buried his face between her legs, tasting her essence with exciting greedy groans. His tongue licked and his fingers touched. Lazarus penetrated her sex, using his fingers to drive her to the edge. Ivy moved her hips, pressing herself more intimately against his lips as he licked at her clit. She cried out as each sensation assaulted her body in heated waves, and she tangled her fingers in his hair as she came, grinding her sex against his face.

"I want you inside me, now. Now!" she demanded.

"Mmmm, assertive, I like that." Lazarus kissed her hard, and she tasted her essence on his lips.

He reached down and pulled her legs up on his shoulders before pressing his cock into her waiting pussy. His groan mixed with her cry of ecstasy as her hot body accepted every inch of him.

"God yes, I am so full of you." She grabbed his hair and pulled his head to hers so she could kiss him before demanding, "Take me hard, don't stop."

Lazarus pumped himself inside her in deep strokes, pushing himself to the hilt and driving her need higher. She was hot and slick for him, and the sensation of this thick length caused her such pleasure she could hardly stand it. She moved her legs and wrapped them around his waist so he could meet her thrust. Their bodies were slick with sweat, and Ivy could hear the wet sound they made as their bodies met.

"You are so hot and tight, princess, I don't want to hurt you," Lazarus groaned harshly.

"You never do, you're my perfect fit," she gasped.

"Say my name again, Ivy, tell me you are mine," he ordered her.

"Lazarus, I am yours and you are mine," Ivy said and whimpered. "I'm going to come, oh yes, yes, yes."

It was as if the dam broke within her, and Ivy screamed as her body shook from the intensity of her orgasm. He pounded himself inside her and followed her into the bliss of his release with a loud groan. He fell on his side beside her, and their bodies heaved as they tried to catch their breath.

Ivy took a deep, cleansing breath and willed her heart to slow to its steady beat. The passion of what they'd just shared burned off most of the alcohol in her system, and she was definitely feeling more sober. Thinking back to how many times she should have been wasted on her ass drunk when she was growing up and rebelling, Ivy understood that her second nature probably had an effect on her metabolism even then.

"You're thinking hard and that's not part of basking in the afterglow," he murmured and kissed her shoulder.

Ivy smiled, rolled over, and placed her head on his chest. "Should I point out we are on the floor? Also, we seem to end up here a lot."

"We can glow where ever we like." Lazarus

chuckled huskily, and she loved hearing the sound rumble through his chest beneath her ear. "I'd like to counter that point with the fact that you tackled me and started to take my clothes off. I couldn't refuse."

She snorted. "Sure you couldn't."

He moved easily off the floor with her in his arms and laid her on the bed. Lazarus nestled himself between her legs and with a slow thrust filled her again. She met his gaze as a gasp escaped her lips.

"I didn't say we were done, did I?" he asked before bending his head to suck her nipple between his lips.

"Oh god, yes," Ivy whimpered.

"You are going to be so amazing as your white wolf," he muttered and lifted her legs high around his waist.

"How did you know it…"

She lost her train of thought as he pumped into her hard and sent her pleasure spiraling upward. Ivy clenched her fingers into the tight muscles of his ass and rode the waves of passion with him. *I'll think about all of it tomorrow,* she promised herself hazily before a soft cry escaped her lips under Lazarus's expert touch.

Chapter Ten

She spent the rest of the weekend with Lazarus and finally accepted the fact that she was his mate. The truth of her parentage began to sink in, and yet she still worried about Eric who had followed through with his threat. Their father had come home to find all of Eric's things gone, and he'd taken exactly half of the money out of the account. He was gone, and they didn't know where to find him.

"Don't worry, Dad, he will come home," she promised over the telephone.

But even as she said it, Ivy didn't believe her words and chewed her lip worriedly because she doubted that would be the case. Lazarus put out feelers to try to find him to make sure he was okay, but that didn't stop her from worrying about her brother who now felt like he had no one in the world but himself.

In the midst of this, Ivy also became impetuous and said yes to Lazarus's offer. She would be moving into his home and moving her art space to the guest house across from the pool. Lazarus had promised not to push her into a change, and if it happened it did, if not she would be fine either way. So now as she parked in front of her loft space, she looked up at it fondly. She would be keeping it and not putting it on the market, because if Eric ever came home, he would have his own space. But today she was going to begin to pack, and a few of Lazarus's pack were going to come by and help her move her stuff to the house on the hill.

She was surprised to see Trent waiting outside her loft door with a sullen expression on his face. This was the first time Ivy had set eyes on him since the incident with her painting. They stared at each other for a long while before Ivy made the first step forward.

"Trent, how are you?" Ivy asked gently.

"I'm good. I'm so sorry for what I did but I miss you," he said quickly.

"Come in, we'll talk inside," she answered and moved past him to unlock the door.

Inside she saw that boxes had been delivered, per her request, and they were stacked neatly against the wall next to her apartment entrance.

"Moving some canvasses to a gallery?" Trent asked.

"No, I don't have a show." Ivy took a deep

breath and turned to him. "I'm moving in with Lazarus."

Trent blanched. "Tell me you're kidding."

"No, I'm not. A lot has gone on since we haven't spoken," she replied.

"Ivy, you can't move in with him. His father killed your mother, and he knew about it," Trent said. "I've found out a lot, too."

She shook her head in confusion. "Wait, what are you talking about?"

"I know you wouldn't believe me, but I had a feeling about him," Trent began. "I started to do my own investigation and found a man who knew your parents and the Vale's. He had documents. Ivy, you're the last descendant of the African white wolf royal family."

"I know that, Dad told me, but what about Lazarus's father killing my mother?" Ivy said, still not believing what Trent was saying.

Trent pulled out papers from his satchel, put them on the small counter of her kitchen, and spread them out. It was ancestry papers and documents that looked legal and old.

"When your mother moved here, apparently she was already pregnant with you. Before you ask, I have no clue who your father is," Trent said. "Lazarus's father found out her secret and all she was worth in Norway and tried to convince her to leave Theo and come with him. Your mother refused, and through the years he tried money and bribes to get her. Finally, he tried to kidnap her and killed her in a fit of anger."

Trent gave her a sad look. "Theo came home to find her dead, but there was no evidence who did it. Look at this report, they said her neck was crushed and had claw marks. This is the real report where witnesses saw Reardon senior leaving the house where you lived. Because of his money and wealth, he was able to get this hidden, and the fake report filed said she died in her sleep from a brain aneurism."

"But that was his father, not Lazarus…" Ivy felt like she was drowning in a depth of despair, and she didn't know how much she could take. "He told me my white wolf would be amazing, but I never told him our ancestry was a white…"

"How would he know that if he just found out after you told him?" Trent pressed. "He knows what his father's done, and he wants everything you are owed due you your heritage. If he can force your wolf out, and it submits to him as the alpha, he owns you Ivy, all that is yours plus your mind, body, and soul."

"He lied?" Ivy whispered, looking at Trent, and her heart shattered in her chest.

Trent laughed hollowly. "He is the Lord and

master in his ivory tower. Just because he got you into bed doesn't mean he started being anything but a man looking to expand his empire by any means necessary."

"I thought I knew him," Ivy said brokenly. "Oh God, what have I done? He'll be expecting me back to the house. He can come here anytime he wants and force me to submit... Oh my God, I can't escape him."

"You need to think. Let's go away for a few days until you can get your head together." Trent pulled her into his arms, and she held on for dear life.

She shook her head frantically. "He can find me, Trent. How can I be with a man who killed my mother?"

"We can try to out run him for a while," Trent said firmly. "We can talk to my friend who gave me this information, and he would know what to do. We can get married, and he couldn't take you from me. We have tons of options, let's just start by getting out of here."

Ivy nodded and wiped the tears that had begun to fall. She thought she knew what betrayal felt like, but she was wrong. She had fallen in love with Lazarus, and he had an ulterior motive from the very beginning.

"Go grab some things, shove them in a bag

and we can leave. We will take my car and leave the city for a while," Trent said.

"Thank you for being here, for telling me the truth." Ivy looked up at him gratefully. "You've always been my best friend, never steered me wrong, wanted nothing from me, just our friendship. I should've trusted you more than I did. I'm sorry I didn't take your warning."

He hugged her quickly. "I'm going to always have your back, Ivy. Now let's get going."

Ivy hurried to the bedroom and didn't even look as she shoved clothes in a bag. She was sure nothing matched, and she probably had no underwear in there. She didn't even try to take her make-up and toiletries. She'd worry about that later, right now they had to run, and it was literally for her life. When she came out of the room, Trent was pressing the disconnect button on his cell phone.

"We'll meet with my friend outside of San Francisco," Trent said. "He'll give us a place to hide out until we figure out what to do."

"What about your practice and your clients?" Ivy asked.

"Nothing is more important than you, Ivy." Trent chucked her under the chin. "Besides, the lawyer side of my life is pretty slow. I need a break. Let's go, bestie."

She gave him a small smile. "Okay… maybe I should call Lazarus and let him tell me his side of the story."

"If you do that, he'll know our plan and be on us like a pack of… for lack of a far better word, wolves," Trent said. "You don't want to give him that advantage."

"You're right," Ivy said. "Thanks for helping me see this clearly. He can't deny the evidence you have."

In the car, she watched the landscape change as they left San Francisco, and she recalled when Lazarus took her to his pack grounds. The paperwork showed it all, that she was just a pawn in a game that was started long before she was born. But he used love to capture her heart, and that made the lies all the worse.

Along the coastline in a small town called Morro Bay, Trent pulled off the road. By that time evening had fallen, and she'd watched the sunset behind the water. Lazarus had to know she was gone by now. Luckily, she had not become one of the pack where he could follow the pack bond to find her. Every time she thought about him, his kiss, his eyes as he cupped her cheek in bed, her heart broke a little more. He could've had everything he wanted, the lands, the titles, everything, if he had just been truthful. But his deception made it that she could never trust him again. Her attention was brought back to the present when Trent stopped the car and parked close to the docks.

"Why are we here?" Ivy asked.

"We need to sleep. We've been traveling for hours," Trent said. "We are meeting Martin here, and we can sleep, eat, and rest."

"There are no hotels around here," Ivy replied looking around.

He took her head and turned it gently. "We're going out on a boat tied up at the dock we can use."

She looked at the lighthouse that sat in the midst of the jagged rocks. The one lone light cut through the darkness but seemed too dim to help. Apprehension filled Ivy as she stepped onto the boat with her luggage but she could see the merit of going to the lighthouse. Even if Lazarus came through town and scented her, he wouldn't find her and would assume they abandoned the car. Wolves had an exceptional sense of smell but it couldn't cross water. In the dim light, the red and white paint on the lighthouse seemed old. They docked, and Trent helped her from the boat. As she got closer, she could see that some of the walls held evident cracks.

"Are you sure this place is safe?" Ivy asked doubtfully. "It seems dilapidated."

"It's out of service. A new one is on Morro Bay, but this makes a great hiding place. Don't let the looks fool you, these things were built to last," Trent explained as they went up the steps.

"If you say so." Ivy made sure not to touch the rusted railing in case it gave way and she went over the edge, breaking her bones on the jagged rocks. She shuddered at the thought.

At the door, Trent knocked loudly, and the sound was hollow in the silence. She pressed herself against the wall away from the rails praying to God someone opened the door quickly. Like Alcatraz, this place gave her the creeps. It was almost like she could hear the echoes of the past, the sounds of ships hitting the rocks and sailors going to their watery graves. *Morbid much,* she thought to herself but breathed a sigh of a relief when the door opened.

Trent took her hand. "Here we go, Ivy."

Inside she expected lights and a shiny gleam that belied the exterior of the lighthouse. She was sadly mistaken because everything inside was old, and what wasn't covered with rags was covered in dust. The silent person led them up more stairs to a second set of rooms. She couldn't see his face through the lantern. He only turned and spoke when they were in a room on the top floor. She could see the light beacon pass by on every turn at the windows.

"This is her," the old man said knowingly as he turned on the light. "I can sense it in her."

Ivy took in his features, an unshaven man with broad shoulders. Even though he was older, he still looked younger than her father. She didn't like his eyes—they reminded her of black coal and showed no emotion within the depths.

"We can't stay here tonight," she said abruptly. "Thanks for telling us what you know but after we are heading back to the mainland."

"The accommodations not suited to you, Princess?" He laughed.

She didn't like the sound and stepped closer to Trent. "Who are you?"

"Allow me to introduce myself," the older man bent at the waist formally. "I'm Martin Moore."

She instantly recognized the name, and she stepped away from Trent, looking at both with wide eyes. The first slivers of fear leached into her veins and turned her blood cold.

"Your father?" Ivy directed her question to Trent. "What the hell is going on?"

"What's going on is that you are exactly where your mother should've been many years ago, with me," Martin replied. "Trent did very well luring you away with the papers I gave him."

"They're not real?" Ivy asked.

Martin paced the room casually. "Some are, conveniently stolen from Lazarus Vale's home. I scented you there that night and almost thought to take you but this way was much better."

"You were there that night," Ivy said knowingly and turned to her true betrayer, Trent. "Why? I thought we were friends."

"Like I said, the lawyer stuff isn't working out." Trent shrugged. "We are the chimera, and we are tired of the scraps the districts offer us. Now with you we have lands, titles, money, we can take our rightful place and own a piece of this city — not even a piece, a nice big chunk. It won't be so bad, you'll be married to me."

Ivy laughed incredulously. "A few things you forgot to factor in, Trent. You can't collect if I don't shift. They won't give me anything without me being able to prove who I am, and even then there may be a fight for the lands from the other pack my mother was to marry into. An alpha is the only one who can cause me to shift, and that was Lazarus — only him. I felt it every time he touched me, kissed me, when he was with his pack. You, Trent, are a spineless freak of nature. You think you can make me shift, you can't even make yourself accept your chimera."

Martin laughed. "Quite right my dear, Trent is certainly no alpha. That is where I come in."

"Dad, she's to be mine!" Trent shouted

"You think you are deserving of a queen?" Martin roared. "You brought her here at my behest, these were my plans. You couldn't even do that right. Vale had her in his bed. She will be my bride."

Ivy laughed again, deciding that bravery in the light of fear was the best way to go. She could not be seen as meek—not now. Lazarus had to have time to find her. "Isn't this nice, two Chimera mutts thinking they can bring out my second nature. Sorry old man, but royalty would never submit to a pack of dogs."

Martin moved quicker than she expected. He grabbed her shoulders and was so close to her face she could smell his breath. "I have my ways, princess. Your mother denied me and look where it got her. She died, clawing for breath under my fingers as you watched. I saw you in the doorway holding your brother and waited, waited for the years to be eaten up and go by as you grew. I knew that this would be the inevitable result, another royal in my arms, one that I could train to submit."

"Never," she whispered.

"Like I said, I have my ways." Martin's smile was filled with malice. "Our children will be marvelous."

"No!" Trent yelled as he rushed forward. "She is mine."

He pushed his father away, and Ivy was shoved against a wall. She hit her head and pain bloomed from the back of her skull as she slid to the floor. Her vision blurred as she watched Trent try to shift to his chimera. His father was already in form because unlike his son he had embraced his second nature. He rushed at Trent with a snarl from a jagged, misshapen jaw.

It was almost in slow motion as Trent's face in a partial shift looked at her on the floor just before he crashed through the window of the lighthouse. Ivy knew that his body would be broken on the rocks below, and his second nature couldn't save him. She felt sadness assail her, knowing she had lost her friend twice that night—once when he betrayed her, and now because he was certainly dead. Martin turned toward her and shifted seamlessly as he walked toward her. Ivy tried to struggle to her feet but the blow to her head made her dizzy and nauseous. Martin laughed at her and stepped back to watch. She felt herself descending into the darkness of her mind and his words sounded far away.

"Time to bring the white wolf to surface," Martin said.

It was the last thing she heard before unconsciousness took hold.

Chapter Eleven

"I can't feel her!" Lazarus roared and punched the wall of her loft.

He knew something was wrong when he came home and didn't find her there. He thought she got sidetracked with an art piece and lost track of time. Not wanting to crowd her, he gave her space, but as the hours ticked by, he decided to go to the loft himself. The scent of the mutt was his first sign of trouble. Her room looking like it was tossed in a crime was the second. Lazarus called Silvia, Luca, and Mikal who made their way to the loft. Lazarus reached out through the power of his alpha's bond and could not feel her. If she was close, he would have felt a hint of her. Since they mated, he always had a sense of her, just a hint, and even that was gone. He missed it, missed her, and his wolf roared in displeasure. He wanted to tear the world apart to find her.

"Lazarus, you need to calm down," Silvia said with worry in her voice.

He whirled on her, and she stepped back in a hurry. His anger went out along the pack bonds and dropped them to their knees. He watched his people begin to shift and took a deep breath trying to calm himself. If he couldn't control himself, his people would begin their shift, at their jobs, homes, parties, and their lives would be in an uproar because the secret would be out. *Protect the pack,* he thought and willed his wolf to be silent. Promising to let him tear the chimera mutt limb from limb when they were found.

"They left by car, not hers but his." Mikal got to his feet and rolled his shoulders as if shaking off the power of the bond that flowed through them. "There is no way to track him."

"Why would she leave with him?" Lazarus said.

"I don't mean to piss you off but maybe it was under duress," Silvia said. "The bedroom looks like chaos ensued."

"Then they die," Lazarus said. "All who helped him will die."

Luca walked away when his phone rang and spoke for a few moments. He turned to Lazarus. "The mutt is at the house, pretty bloody, very hurt, jabbering about his father."

"Tell whoever is on that phone keep him alive," Lazarus ordered and strode toward the door with the three of them on his heels. "I need to know what he knows then I'll kill him."

Silvia got into his car and he pulled off before she had the door closed fully. He watched from the corner of his eye as she tightened the seatbelt and held on to the door with a white knuckled grasp. He understood his driving wasn't the safest at that point but every second that ticked by, he felt Ivy was in more danger. He made the trip to the house in half the time it usually took, and he hopped out of the car as soon as he stopped.

"Lazarus! Lazarus! Don't kill him until we get the information," Silvia yelled as she struggled to get the seatbelt off, and he heard her yell. "Fucking useless seatbelt!"

In the house, they had put Trent in the kitchen, and he was lying on a sleeping bag. Lazarus looked down at him mercilessly. His breathing was even but his leg, and probably his arm, was broken. He had a second nature, and the chimera did heal even though not as quickly as the wolves did. Still, if he didn't get those bones set quickly, it would heal as is and probably not well. Lazarus had no pity for the man as he dragged him up and shook him like a rag doll. He had a sense of pleasure as Trent cried out in pain.

"Lazarus, stop shaking the mutt and let him talk. Ivy is our priority," Silvia said as she walked in. "Besides, his cries are annoying, and I want to kill him myself."

Lazarus brought the whimpering Trent toward his face and snarled, "Talk!"

"He thinks I'm d—dead," Trent said pitifully with tears running down his face. "I didn't think…"

"Who thinks you're dead?" Lazarus asked and dropped him back to the ground. "Christ, wipe your face and act like a man."

"My father thinks I'm dead. He pushed me through a window so he could take Ivy for himself, he thinks he can force her wolf from within and then marry her and get the titles she owns," Trent explained.

"What?" Lazarus roared and surged toward him. If it wasn't for his pack restraining him, Lazarus knew he would have snapped Trent's neck.

"Don't let him hurt me," Trent whimpered and scrabbled to the corner.

Luca crouched in front of him like he was a child and said gently, "No one will hurt you but we need to know about Ivy."

"Don't make promises you can't keep, Luca," Lazarus snarled.

"We lied to her, told her that Vale Senior killed her mother," Trent explained weakly. He kept a wary eye on Lazarus in case he broke free of those who held him. "I didn't know it was actually my father who did that until much later. We wanted to give the chimera a leg up in this game, a real standing in the districts."

"You had that until your people tried to play a deadly game," Lazarus reminded him.

"So we should be punished for the rest of our existence?" Trent cried out. "I wanted to help my pack, my family."

"You chimera always go about things the wrong fucking way," Lazarus yelled. "Why not petition the packs, gather people on your side? Hell, Ivy was already asking me to look into it for you, and I was going to do it, for her. Because I love her, she is my mate, and you took her to gain a foothold?"

Lazarus surged forward again and Trent tried to get smaller in the corner. "You're right, she was—is my best friend, and I used her. Then my father used us both. He was willing to see me die to have her. He killed her mother, and Ivy saw it all."

"Where does he have her?" Luca asked and put a firm but gentle hand on Trent's shaking shoulder as the chimera cried.

"The old lighthouse off Morro Bay. We took a boat out there," Trent said. "He pushed me hard out the window, and I hit the rocks but mostly water. I swam some and let the tide take me in so he wouldn't know I was alive. I drove straight here."

"Get Doc to come patch him up," Lazarus ordered. "I want him taken to the pack grounds and held there. That way if anything is wrong with Ivy, I can have a good and proper hunt."

"What do you mean?" Trent asked.

Lazarus crouched down until they were eye level. "What it means is that if one hair on her head is harmed in any way, I will let you free to run, and I will chase you until you're exhausted. Then I will snap your neck between my jaws, taste your blood, watch you struggle for breath and the light leave your eyes as you die. Then I will tear you apart, I won't eat your flesh. No you are not worthy of being food for any wolf. But I will scatter you so there is nothing to bury and let whatever animal feed on your carcass."

"Well shit, that's more than a little disturbing," Mikal mumbled.

"Can we take the cars..." Silvia began.

"No, we run, it's quicker. Get Stone or Jamie to drive the van up there to bring us home," Lazarus said. "He may have brought others to protect the lighthouse by now."

"Then we go in ready to fight," Luca said with determination.

"We go in ready to kill for our Alpha's mate," Silvia said.

"His father is mine." Lazarus turned to look at Trent. "I hope you made your peace with the man somewhere inside you because he won't live past tonight."

Trent met his gaze. "To me he's already dead."

When Doc arrived with others to escort Trent to the pack grounds, Lazarus and those going with him gave themselves over to the wolf within. The gut wrenching need to hunt and to find his mate overtook Lazarus, and his wolf released a howl of distress and anger. The black wolf was furious at being withheld for so long, and the suffering of his mate was in his mind as he ran. He moved through the trees and could hear the soft footfalls of his pack as they tried to keep up. Tonight he would taste the blood of his enemy in his throat.

The electric current ran through her and caused

the muscles in her body to go rigid and spasm painfully. Ivy couldn't help the scream of pain that escaped her lips as Martin tried to torture her wolf free. This was phase two of his mission to bring out her white wolf. He had tried to force his will on her but as a chimera it was laughable because it had no effect. Then he tried to make her submit and get between her legs. Ivy fought like a wild cat, scratching and screaming. She bit him and kicked him between the legs. He wouldn't let his people in to help because he would look weak, and in his anger this was his final attempt.

"Give in, I can see it running along your skin," Martin said harshly and slapped her cheek hard.

The sting, combined with his torture, had Ivy gasping for breath. "That wasn't the wolf, that was my revulsion for you."

Martin grabbed her face cruelly. "You think this is a game, Princess? Maybe I'll have a few of the bigger chimera come in here and take you against your will, ravage you until your wolf is forced to defend. Maybe that benefits me because as your body is torn so will your mind."

"I will bite every dick off and spit it on the floor," Ivy said even though the idea was so vile she had to force herself not to retch in disgust. "You'd better kill me and run, old man, because when Lazarus finds you there won't be enough of you left to bury."

"How will he find you?" Martin laughed.

"Maybe in our mating we connected, and I'm part of his pack's bond now?"

Ivy smiled and then cried out in pain as he turned on the electricity in revenge for her words. Lying on the old, musty bed was not one of the things that was on her to-do list. But as she gasped for breath, she goaded him on, hoping to buy enough time for Lazarus to find her.

"You never know. Lazarus is more of a man than you or your son could ever be. Maybe he activated a part of my wolf mentally, and now he's following it here. He's going to kill you, you know." Ivy wished with all her heart she could feel him, that she could tell him she was okay.

"He will find a surprise on this small island if and when he shows up," Martin snapped. "And if he makes it to me, then you'll watch me kill that pup. I've learned a few things in my lifetime."

Ivy wrinkled her nose. "Obviously not good skincare or a bath regimen. You smell like a wet dog."

He turned on the power again, and she started to scream this time because it was way higher than before. It burned the skin at her wrist as the current caused her to thrash on the old bed. When he turned it off, she pretended to be unconscious, knowing he would wait a while for her to wake up. Martin slapped her face hard, and she didn't flinch. She needed for him to think she had passed out. Martin shoved her face away with a grunt of anger, and she heard him move across the floor with slow, shuffling steps. *Viable my ass, Lazarus is going to kill the hell out of you,* she thought. *Hear me,* she whispered mentally pushing her thoughts with intensity, hoping he'd pick them up. She kept begging within her mind, *Lazarus, love, please find me, find me, find me.*

Ivy? It was like a whisper in the wind, barely there but she knew she heard it, and her heart leapt in joy. *Lazarus, find me, lighthouse, I hear you! I love you!* She heard him again, and it was strong this time when he answered, *I'm coming baby.* It had never happened before but their connection was there. She had to hold on just a little longer, just a bit more. She snuck a peek at Martin and saw him in the corner chugging water, and he slammed the plastic bottle down on the old table hard. Ivy closed her eyes quickly as he came over with the bottle and poured water all over her face. She stayed still as possible even as some ran into her nose, and she wanted to cough and gag so badly. Someone walked in the room, and she kept her eyes closed as this man with a deep voice spoke to Trent's father.

"Is she dead?"

"Damn it, maybe too much current in that jolt. She's out cold, I'll have to wait until she regains consciousness," Martin muttered.

"Hopefully you didn't fry her brain. You can't get her money and stuff if she's a vegetable," the man with the deep voice chortled.

Martin snarled and practically yelled, "Just do your job and patrol the damn island in case the wolves come for her."

"They'll meet up with more than they realize if they do show their dog faces here. We are stronger and faster than the old chimera," the man said. "We will rip them limb from limb and leave the water red with their blood."

A lone howl echoed in the wind and came through the broken window. Ivy's heart leapt with excitement because she could also hear the sound of a boat engine through the window, getting closer.

"It seems you'll get your chance to show your worth after all," Martin said. "Kill them all."

She heard the hurried footfalls leave the room and then listened as Martin paced the floor. He stopped when the sounds of a fight started, the snarls of angry wolves and the cries of the chimera being killed with methodical viciousness. She needed to take his focus away from the battle outside. The black wolf would be coming to find her and to kill him.

"How does it feel knowing that you will die today?" Ivy asked. "I can see from your face the battle is not going well."

"He can't get in here." Martin turned to her and started to unbuckle one of her hands. "Wolves can't open doors and there is only one into this building, or so everyone thinks. I think it's time for us to go, Princess."

As soon as her hands were released, she tried to claw his face even though the burns at her wrist were painful. He held on to the wounds and squeezed until she cried out. A howl came clearly through the broken window, and she could hear the sound of something climbing the walls outside. Martin moved away quickly not even trying to shed his clothes as he shifted, instead letting them be torn apart as the chimera in him broke free.

The black wolf, her Lazarus, propelled himself through the window, and she wondered how because the side of the wall was a steep incline. Martin, now in his chimera form, bared his teeth, the lips of his ragged, deformed jaw peeling back to show sharp, yellowing incisors.

The black wolf cast her a glance and attacked without any show of fear. Ivy watched as the chimera tried to sink its teeth in Lazarus's black fur and yelped when Lazarus dug his claws into Martin's mangy, calico coat. She watched blood ooze from the open wounds, and Martin sounded like a wounded pup as Lazarus bit the back of his neck and tossed him against the wall. She worked at then restraint on the other hand and then her ankles quickly, looking at the prone body of her attacker revert slowly back to human form on the ground. *Not changing,* she heard it clearly in her head as she moved toward him, and Ivy smiled.

"Oh my god, I heard that." She laughed huskily. "I could hear you in my head, low at first, and I knew you were coming."

Lazarus's attention was on her, and she walked over to him. The sound of the shot echoed in the room. Ivy saw Lazarus's body jerk, and his black fur instantly became wet as he slumped against the floor.

"Lazarus!" Ivy screamed and rushed forward, putting her hand on his fur. When she lifted her hand, it was covered with blood.

"If I can't have you, he certainly won't," Martin said in a feeble, rasping voice.

"No!" She heard the shrillness of her own

voice, and Lazarus's breathing was shallow underneath his fur.

Something seemed to break free inside her. She looked back at Martin with malice in her eyes. Ivy felt the new sensation crawl along her skin and down to her fingertips. She slapped her palms face down and curled her fingers into claws on the ground as she panted hard. Her lungs felt like they were constricting in her chest, and her muscles rippled. Her arms shortened, and her jaw shifted, breaking and contorting to form new features. There was no pain, just the rearrangement of bones that seemed to crack and shift silently under skin that felt like soft pin pricks all over as fur sprouted from her skin. It seemed to take forever but was over in moments. Ivy shook herself and looked down to see a white paw. Her second nature had made an appearance. So enthralled by her shift and her beauty, Martin watched her as she stalked toward him slowly. The gun he used to shoot Lazarus like a coward clattered from his fingers.

"You are truly magnificent." He said in awe and reached out to touch her.

Ivy bit at his hand, refusing to let the man who shot her mate soil her with his touch. She looked down at him and felt no pity as she placed her large paw in the center of his chest.

"Do it," Martin whispered, and Ivy obliged. She bit his neck and felt the blood as she pierced his skin with her teeth. She ripped the skin, tore the veins, and watched his blood flow and his eyes become devoid of life as he stared up at the white glorious wolf.

Mine, she heard the voice in her head and turned quickly to see Lazarus stand on shaky legs. There was a thump, and the bullet clattered on the floor as his body expelled it.

Mine, she repeated the word and moved over to nuzzle his neck. *Not dead, not lost*

His voice was clear and comforting, like a blanket in her mind, when he spoke again. *No, found.*

He didn't even spare Martin a glance as he walked over to the window, and she followed. He was larger than her and put his paws on the windowsill and jumped out easily from the window to the flat grass far below the window. The black wolf looked up at her, and without fear Ivy followed her mate and landed easily beside him. His pack gathered around, and Ivy felt their awe as they nuzzled her softly in acceptance. Lazarus raised his head and howled into the night, and Ivy raised her voice with his. The other wolves bowed their heads in acceptance of her new dominant role as mate to their alpha before they added their voices to the howl that echoed across the water and into the night.

Chapter Twelve

Ivy was caught in a whirlwind of activity and yet she had no problem with all that was going on. Two weeks after the incident in Morrow Bay, she was moved in with Lazarus, the threat of the chimera was thwarted, and she was standing in front of her mate with her hands in his as they got married on pack grounds. Her shift to wolf became easier the more she did it, and as she understood the white wolf within her, she found that its personality was instinct, primal and carnal, protection of home and those she loved, honor and pack bonds.

She felt the connection with the pack now more than ever, and they were in one perfect unity. The mating bond she shared with Lazarus was the strongest aspect that she loved and never wanted to be without. If he moved from their bed, she knew instantly and was trying to get accustomed to knowing his whereabouts at all times. He encouraged her to sleep even if he moved, hoping to teach her to ignore the feelings sometimes. But yet each time she woke up to protect her mate.

For her wedding, the alphas of each district were invited so they could see their mating and know that if anyone tried to hurt her to get to Lazarus, they would meet with a very harsh end. Trent represented the chimera, and after they returned home, Lazarus gave her the choice of what should be done with him. The offer floored Ivy because Lazarus giving her the choice, knowing full well he would not lose any sleep over snapping Trent's neck, showed more love than most realized. In the end, he was allowed to live because the devil they knew was better than the one they didn't. Trent would now lead the chimera, and they would be given more resources for his people. But if he stepped out of line, Trent would always know that Lazarus the black wolf watched from the darkness, blending into the shadows.

"I'm sorry, Ivy, I am so very sorry for my part in what my father did," Trent said after the decision was made. "I hope we can still be friends."

Ivy met his eyes. Any feelings she had for him were gone. "I may have saved your life, Trent, but it wasn't because of friendship. You lived because your people need a leader, nothing more.

Whatever we had died in that room with your father. You mean nothing to me, and if you fuck it up, I won't save you twice."

After the wedding they would be honeymooning in Norway and then to Africa, traveling with Luca, Mikal, and Silvia. It was time to reclaim her home and titles. They had already sent formal notice to the clans in Norway, and a reception would be held in her honor. They wanted to see that she was real, and she was ready for them. Her second nature had given her a new strength, and she wanted to avenge her mother who'd had to run because of love. She wanted to know who killed her father, for they would pay. Her father had already spoken to her about whom he thought was the culprit since Agnor had spoken about the man extensively.

He would also be going with them. It would be the first time Theo had stepped foot in Norway in the thirty-one years since meet her mother and her true father. But she focused on the man who stood in front of her wearing a charcoal suit that only accentuated his dark sexy looks and wicked grin. She was the white wolf, and she smiled in return recalling how he looked at her and laughed out loud when she walked into the circle of their pack. She chose a black wedding dress instead of white to pay homage to her mate's wolf coloring.

"White wolf, black wedding dress, I like it," he said in her ear before the service began.

"You didn't expect anything normal for me, right?" Ivy teased.

"What fun would that be," Lazarus replied.

The ceremony was being officiated by Doc, who seemed not only to be the pack doctor but an ordained priest. The final words Doc said sealed them together forever, and she felt it them deep in her heart.

"Lazarus, she is wife, mother to the pack and your children, your mate, and the beat of your heart. Do you accept her as such?" Doc asked.

"I do," Lazarus answered automatically.

"Ivy, he is husband, alpha to the pack as he is father to them and your children, your mate, and the beat of your heart. Do you accept him as such?" Doc asked her.

"I do, very much so," Ivy answered.

"Then the bonds are sealed, never to be broken. Hundreds of years may go by but may you forever be held in love and mated," Doc said. "What say you, pack?"

A howl went up among the people, and he took her lips in a kiss as she clung to his shoulders greedily tasting him in return. As the party started, they sat at the head picnic table, with Silvia and Luca always there for protection. The leaders of each district were escorted away, not allowed to stay for the celebration, and that included Trent who smiled at her and got nothing in return. Ivy felt the glare of someone and scented their anger, she was stronger than most thought, and she turned her head instantly to the source.

"Will you excuse me?" Ivy said sweetly, lifting her dress easily as she moved.

"Ivy?" Silvia warned gently.

"Let her be," Lazarus said casually and took a bite of his food. "They need to know she will never hide behind me."

Ivy took the seat across from Raven and met her gaze. "Problem?"

Raven gave her a thin smile. "No, you are the mate of our alpha, why would I have a problem?"

"Maybe because you want to be where I am," Ivy replied. "But you are right, I'm his mate, and I have his heart. He is mine, not yours, never will be yours, and you will never have him. Find another man to fixate on because honey, I will bite your throat out for mine. Enjoy the party."

Ivy went back to her seat and Lazarus kissed her hard. "Well done. I do love when you are assertive."

"Anything for you, you are my love and my mate," Ivy said return. "P.S... I'll show you assertive later."

"Ugh, did not need to hear that," Silvia muttered.

After their meal, and when the moon was full, the pack shed their clothes without embarrassment and took to the tree line to run. This time she kept up with the black wolf, and they moved so quickly they were almost a blur as they led the pack of wolves through the dense woods under the moonlight.

Okafor Fortress, originally named Oscarsborg, was nestled on one of the two small islands. Across on the mainland was the small town of Drebak. The Norwegian military had taken over the fortress at one point. But the Oscarsborg family had taken it back and willed it to her grandfather who named it Okafor to remind the clan of their roots. Okafor was part of the lands of her mother's heritage. That was who she was and the blood that ran through her veins. Her mother was Zoya Okafor, her father was Agnor Sakebo, and she was the last white wolf of the Okafor clan.

When they arrived in Norway, she held her father's hand tight as they traveled to Drebak, where she claimed all that was hers that had been placed in a trust. She watched him cry and held him as silent tears flowed when they arrived at the fortress. To her it was more of a castle but to him it was the last piece of the memories shared with him by his friends. Then Zoya became the woman he loved and protected as best he could, and together they raised two children. It held happiness and sorrow, and for the first time Ivy understood. Theo not only grieved for her mother but her true father as well, every day for all the years that had past.

"I feel them here, together and happy," he said brokenly. "Oh, how I wish they had a chance for happiness in this life."

"Dad, they loved you. They look at us now, and they are smiling thinking well done, Theo Bellefonte our true friend." Ivy wiped her own tears. "There has never been a better father than you. Thank you for watching over me and protecting both me and Eric even though your heart was broken."

Ivy held her dad tight and wished Eric was there, but he hadn't even come for her wedding because no one knew where to find him. Now he was missing the first look at their mother's home.

She still had to be presented to the clans that were now left who still did not believe she was who she said she was. But to receive what was in her trust, she had to shift for the trustee. She had worn her mother's necklace from the time her father placed it around her neck at the airport.

With Theo to verify and all the letters her mother left, she was more than prepared to face the bastards who may have killed her father. As she looked out the window across the water into the night and the lights of houses in Drebak, she sat with the final letter from her mother in her hand. Again, Theo had given it to her when their feet touched Norway and told her to read it before they met with the clan that night. So while Lazarus and his enforcers made sure she was safe, she opened the envelope that had yellowed with age and pulled out the folded paper from inside. She read the words, and for a moment she could hear her mother's voice in her head.

My dearest Ivy,

I can only imagine your beauty as you stand in our family home. I wonder if you would have been a different girl if you were raised in Africa or Norway? I doubt it, because from the time of your birth you were always filled with a fire that could never be doused. Even your cries were spirited at your birth, and I knew that it would be you who carried the bloodline of the white wolf. My Eric has it within him too, but his coloring will be that of a mixed blood child, not pure. I hope he doesn't hate me for this someday for all we did to protect you. I hope he is with you now, standing facing those who played God with our lives.

When you face the council be brave. If they feel you are weak, they will try to take your life. Protect your father, because if I know Theo, he will come with you, and they will say he stole you away, us away. Nothing was further from the truth, without him we would have been dead. Theo is the bravest man to travel with us and take on a cause not his. Without a doubt, he chose to protect and love us like we were his own. Stay true to yourself, love hard and wisely, protect yours with the fierceness of the white wolf within you. Be blessed in all you do, my precious daughter.

Your Mother,
Zoya

Mom. Ivy traced the beautiful writing with her fingers and read the letter again before lifting it to her nose and inhaling the fading scent. At that point, she longed for the woman she could barely remember and wished that she was standing with them now. Ivy thought about everything as she stared at the moon over the water. If she had grown up here, she'd probably have never met Lazarus. He opened the door to the bedroom that they chose to sleep in and she turned with a smile as he walked to her.

"Luca and Silvia are outside the door, ready to go downstairs?" Lazarus asked.

"I feel like a diplomat under secret service protection," Ivy said. "Is this all necessary?"

"We know what extent they tried to go to in regard to your mother," Lazarus answered. "There is no way they get the opportunity to harm you."

"They wouldn't have a chance, I have my black wolf husband with me." She smiled up at him.

"My Ivy, the moon is jealous in its sky right now because I can touch you and all it can do is caress your skin with the light." Lazarus ran his finger over her bottom lip.

"My, my, since when did you become a poet?" Ivy teased.

"Since I've been exploring this place. Every tapestry on the wall has some kick ass saying on it." Lazarus grinned. "Your people were smooth operators in the day."

"Nice, you stole the pretty words you just said to me." Ivy pretended to pout.

He kissed her gently. "It doesn't matter where

I got them, just as long as they come from the heart to you."

She wrapped her arms around his neck. "Good point."

There was a soft knock on the door and with her fingers laced in his Ivy went to the door. Silvia, dressed in a black pantsuit and stiletto heels, looked as sexy as she was dangerous. Luca didn't have a smile on his face but his wink toward her was one of encouragement. The two enforcers preceded them down the hallway and the massive staircase of Okafor Fortress.

"I count three that give me a sense of unease," Silvia commented as all eyes turned to see them coming down the stairs.

"Anyone looks at her funny they die," Lazarus said mildly not changing his disposition.

Theo was standing at the bottom of the stairs in the large foyer, and he was dressed in a blue business suit. She was so accustomed to her *Da* in regular working clothes that she almost didn't recognize him. Twelve people were in the room, and Ivy chose to speak to them on her terms while standing. They would sense a move if anyone had any bad intentions, and this would go from a meeting to a war.

Lazarus spoke, and his voice was loud and clear. "Ivy Okafor, the last of the royal white wolves, has graciously invited you to her family home tonight. She bids you welcome."

One man stepped forward dressed immaculately in a gray suit with the white collarless shirt beneath buttoned up to his neck with gold ornate buttons.

"George Freiberg Alpha of the *Vill-Skog* pack," he bowed low. *"Velkommen til dine forfedre land."*

His attaché translated. "He said welcome to the lands of your ancestors."

Ivy inclined her head. "Thank you, and I will make an effort to learn the language of my mother's first home in Africa first and foremost. Norwegian will be second, if you are more comfortable speaking in your own dialect."

George gave a thin smile. "English is fine."

Ivy inclined her head. "Now to the business at hand. You've been given proof of who I am and the executor of my family's holding has sent you written notification approving of who I am."

"Yes, and we accept all of this. Are you here to complete the agreement between your people and mine?" George paced slowly before turning to her. He licked his lips and her stomach rolled in revulsion. "A union of our packs with you as the bride?"

Lazarus growled softly. "She is mated to me, there will be no such agreement."

Ivy placed her hand on Lazarus's arm to calm him and felt the muscles bunch beneath her hand.

She met George's gaze coolly. "That agreement was over thirty years ago and was not approved by my mother."

"But it was by your grandfather, and he was leader of the Okafor clan," George cut in.

"Yes he was, and between him and your people, someone killed my father and my mother when they chose to leave," Ivy replied. "To me, it means this arrangement is null and void."

George threw his hands up in the air. "There is not proof of this."

Theo stepped forward and spoke. "I was there, I saw it happen, I helped Zoya escape from New York where we first stayed and went across the country, hiding who she truly was."

"The human friend of Zoya and Agnor Sokebe, who says you didn't kill him to keep her for yourself?" George sneered.

"Who said they were all together when my father was killed?" Ivy shot back. "Unless someone else was witness, the person who killed Agnor, maybe?"

"There have always been stories," George said unabashed. "Rumors of what happened that night in the United States."

Ivy smiled. "Rumors that made it all the way here to Norway? Hmmm, good to know. In any case, since there will be no union or marriage between myself and any of your people, I am here to offer you an alternative."

"A marriage between the clans is all I will accept," George said stubbornly.

"Then you will leave here with nothing," Lazarus spoke up. "It would be best to listen to her offer, because if anyone touches her, I will unleash hell and kill you all without hesitation."

"You are the last of your people, you have no wolf pack to back you," George snapped.

Ivy raised her hand to stop his words. "I have my husband's pack. He and his people outnumber yours. At my behest, if you take this any further, there will be a war and you will lose. My alternative to a union is this: I am willing to sign over the lands that your people live on at no cost. We will count the payments made to the executor of my estates while I was away as payment in full."

"Drebak included," George countered.

Ivy shook her head. "No, I'm not stupid, George Freiberg. I know that Drebak is a tourist hub and where those who live on the Okafor Isles go to buy and sell. We will never barter with you for what is ours. You get the lands you inhabit beyond Drebak and nothing more. Be thankful I offer you that much."

"You presume to take on the airs of a queen," George murmured. "I wonder if you will back up such strong words?"

Ivy met his gaze, and her eyes never wavered. "I will tell you this, George Freiberg, Alpha to the Vill-skog pack. I will defend my words, my mother, the way her father did not. I will bring half of the pack here and fight for what is ours. And trust me when I say it's best to take my offer now, before I begin the investigation on who killed my father. When this happens and the person or persons is found, I will kill them myself. As it is, maybe you should look out for your pack's welfare before your death."

"Very large words…"

Ivy leaned forward. "Try me, sweetie, I dare you."

The rest of the people in the room began to shout, and she couldn't understand the language. George moved over to them and began to yell in return. She looked at Theo who gave her a thumbs up. Even though he didn't understand everything they were saying, they were winning.

Finally, George turned to back to her. "We accept your terms."

"Good, we will have the paper work drawn

up and you can sign in a few days. You'll be contacted then." Ivy smiled. "Good night gentlemen, I trust you know your way home."

With that she turned and left, heading back up the stairs without glancing in the direction of those who had gathered there.

"Good job, sweetheart, they are leaving," Lazarus murmured in her ear. "You don't turn to look. Luca, Mikal, and Silvia will make sure they are gone and then run a security sweep."

"That was the hardest thing I ever had to do," she whispered. Back in the room, she let go of the rigidness of her spine and sat on the bed. "Holy crap, that was intense."

"You were magnificent." Lazarus was busy taking off his jacket and then his shirt.

"What are you doing?" Ivy asked.

"I'm going to have my mate naked beneath me," he explained. "I find that my sweet love has the grit of a true Queen, and it has left me very aroused. So if you don't want to destroy that dress, I suggest you take it off."

His words made her wet and aroused, and as she struggled to take off the satin blue gown, he stalked her like the predator he was. Ivy moved back on the bed as he covered her body with his.

She looked into his eyes. "I do love you so."

"I love you, Ivy."

He kissed her hard and with passion while she ran her hands over the muscular shoulders of his back and arms. He pulled her leg high around his waist, and she felt his hand on the curve of her ass. Lazarus's touch inflamed her, and each new caress was like heat against her skin until she arched silently begging for more. Lazarus lifted his head as he cupped the heavy globes of her breasts. She whimpered and shifted restlessly beneath him as he licked the pert rose-blush tips.

"You are so very responsive, I am addicted to the noises you make," he murmured with assured-ness in his voice. "Do you want my nipples in your mouth?"

"Yes, yes I do, Lazarus please," she whispered urgently.

He obliged her, and she felt his hot mouth enclose one nipple and then the other sucking them deeply between his lips. Pleasure speared through her, and she arched, holding his head against her. Ivy growled softly and bit his shoulder, loving the way he growled in response. He laughed in delight when she flipped him easily on to his back. Ivy kissed her way down his body and took his hard cock in her grasp, stroking firmly and watching his hips rise to meet the movements of her hand.

Their eyes connected, and she loved how his eyes seemed to penetrate her very soul. She never broke their gaze as she lowered her head and took his cock between her soft lips. A low moan escaped him, and she used that sound as a queue to take more of him in her mouth. His hand was in her hair fisting at her scalp and holding her steady so he could glide between her lips. "Ivy." Her name was a harsh sound that escaped his lips. He pulled her up to him savagely and kissed her, rolling until she was beneath him again. Lazarus slipped his hand between them and began to caress the wet flesh of her sex. Ivy spread her legs eagerly anticipating his touch and when he followed the slickness of her slit and entered her with his fingers. She cried out, lifting her hips trying to get them deeper inside her.

"Oh sweetheart you are so hot and wet around my fingers," he said against her lips. "Your scent drives me wild."

Lazarus slipped another finger within her, simulating the thrusting pace of their lovemaking soon to come. She pistoned her hips against his seeking hand feeling her pleasure increase as he found the secret spot within her pussy. She arched as she felt the beginning of her orgasm within her, and she heard the loud carnal sounds she made, amazed that they came from her lips.

His eyes were on her, she could feel his intense gaze, and her breath was released in pants and moans. She was so wet they could hear it between his fingers each time he moved them inside her.

"I'm going to come, Lazarus yes."

She heard the excitement in her own voice, and the exotic scent of his skin and her body filled her nose. He pressed his fingers deeper inside her and bit at her upturned nipples gently. Ivy spiraled into her orgasm and felt him thrust his cock deep inside her as her body quaked. Lazarus groaned when her pussy clenched and spasmed around his cock. The sheer pleasure of it almost sent her careening into another release. She looked up to see the intensity on his face, and he thrust hard inside her. Ivy pulled his head down to kiss him as they caught the rhythm that pulsed between them. He grabbed her hips to still her frantic movements.

"Stop baby, God you're going to make me come if you keep moving like that," Lazarus groaned out, his breathing harsh and his arms tense above her.

She was having a hard time being still. "Come with me, Lazarus, don't hold back."

"I want to make it last... You drive me to distraction," he said huskily. "Is it wrong to want to be buried within you forever, to be frozen in time like this? Looking down at you and seeing the love in your eyes for me?"

She lifted her head and kissed him fiercely. "There will more time like this, a forever like this, because a day won't go by without you knowing how much I love you."

As they kissed, he thrust against her hard and met the lifting of her hips each time she moved. He gripped her hips and pounded into her in a savage frenzy that drove her to cry out his name.

"Now, Lazarus, now!" she cried out.

Her body shook with a pleasure she never thought possible and found only with him. He groaned her name, and it mingled with her cries of ecstasy. As she succumbed to her own release, his hot seed filled her. The wolf within howled in pleasure, and she felt their bond, the one created by love and mating more strongly than ever. In the aftermath, he nuzzled her neck gently, and she nipped at his shoulder. It was more than a few minutes before they spoke using words instead of touch.

"How would you like to run with your mate and explore the Okafor Isle?" she asked suddenly.

"Now?" he murmured and sighed in contentment.

"Please?" she said gently.

He nodded with a smile. "Okay, love."

They found the robes they brought and after telling Silvia and Luca where they would be, Ivy gave her body over to the wolf within and watched Lazarus do the same. The air smelled different, ripe and lush, as they ran over mossy logs and drank from small streams. She could sense the magic on the isle, feel her ancestors within the soil and trees.

Something within her knew this was a second home, and she was excited to see what awaited them in Africa. As she lay with Lazarus in a small grassy knoll and looked at the moon between the trees, she felt more complete than she ever had in her life. Her dark wolf nuzzled her gently, and she teasingly nipped at his neck. She could already feel the inspiration to paint everything she saw and felt with her new senses as her guide. But right now, the white wolf rested, cocooned and warm against the fur of her black wolf mate.

The End

About the Author

Dahlia Rose is the best-selling author of contemporary and paranormal romance with a hint of Caribbean spice. She was born and raised on a Caribbean island and now currently lives in Charlotte, North Carolina, with her four kids, who she affectionately nicknamed "The Children of the Corn," and her biggest supporter and longtime love. She has a love of erotica, dark fantasy, sci-fi, and the things that go bump in the night. Books and writing are her biggest passions, and she hopes to open your imagination to the unknown between the pages of her books.

53395301R00117

Made in the USA
Columbia, SC
17 March 2019